THE SQUEAKY WHEEL

Also by Robert Kimmel Smith

CHOCOLATE FEVER

JELLY BELLY

THE WAR WITH GRANDPA

MOSTLY MICHAEL

BOBBY BASEBALL

THE

SQUEAKY WHEEL

ROBERT KIMMEL SMITH

 Delacorte Press

Published by
Delacorte Press
Bantam Doubleday Dell Publishing Group, Inc.
666 Fifth Avenue
New York, New York 10103

Library of Congress Cataloging in Publication Data

Smith, Robert Kimmel [date of birth]
    The squeaky wheel / by Robert Kimmel Smith.
    p. cm.
    Summary: Moving to a new neighborhood following his parents' divorce, Mark has trouble making new friends and coping with his father's absence.
    ISBN 0-385-30155-3
    [1. Divorce—Fiction. 2. Friendship—Fiction.] I. Title.
PZ7.S65762Sq 1990
[Fic]—dc20   89-77063
                                                      CIP
                                                      AC

Manufactured in the United States of America

October 1990

10 9 8 7 6 5 4 3 2 1
BVG

For Mark, Peter, and Julie

CONTENTS

vii

CONTENTS

1

SCARED AND MAD

This is how the third-worst day of my life began: It was the first day of school and I was late.

Mom had her hand on my shoulder, shaking me out of sleep. "Mark, get up, honey. I must have overslept."

I threw off the blanket as Mom scooted out of the room, then got out of bed onto the bare wood floor. I had that hollow feeling inside like I get before a math test. Even though I was barely awake I knew how I felt: scared and mad.

Scared because not only was it a new school, I wasn't even registered yet and I'd be late.

Mad because I didn't want to be here in this scuzzy apartment and I didn't want to go to a new school. I had about eighty-eight other reasons to be mad as well. In fact, I'd been in a permanent state of mad for about six months.

I rushed to the bathroom in the dark hallway, but Mom was already in there. I could hear the shower running.

Great.

THE SQUEAKY WHEEL

Back in our old house I would have used the bathroom in the hall and Mom would be showering in her old bathroom. Back in our old house there would be carpet on the floor in my room and I'd be going off to school with my friends.

Back in our old house my dad would have been there too.

I walked into the living room, to the window that looks out on Beverly Road, the floor cool under my bare feet. When we'd finished unpacking the movers' cartons, my slippers were nowhere to be found. Now it was Wednesday morning and my feet felt funny.

Across the street in the A & P a few people were already shopping. Sal's pizzeria was closed and so was Mostly Books, next door. A few kids were walking by on their way to school. All of them were strangers.

Scared and mad, that was how my day was starting.

Mom yelled to me when she left the bathroom and I ran in there and did my stuff. I finished by sticking my head under the tap and getting my hair wet. I can't really wake up in the morning unless I wet my hair. Back home I'd have these arguments with Mom about going outside on a cold morning with a wet head.

I got dressed in a hurry and went into the kitchen. Mom was sitting in front of a cup of coffee, staring at it. I gobbled half a bowl of cereal and took two long gulps of a glass of milk. "I hate being late," I said.

"Sorry," Mom said, "my fault. I slept through the alarm." She finally took one sip of her coffee and made a face, then looked me over. "You're not going to school dressed like that?" she said.

I looked at what I had on. A pair of clean jeans and my

Detroit Tigers T-shirt, which was clean but had an ink stain on one sleeve. "Sure I am," I said.

"It's the first day of school," she said.

"So?"

"Don't you want to look your best? On the very first day?"

"No. And there's no time."

"Honey," she said in her wheedling voice, "come on."

"Only dweebs dress up for school," I said.

Mom shot me a look and got up from the table. Then she went into my room and I could hear her opening one of my dresser drawers. She came back into the kitchen with one of my new long-sleeve sport shirts. As she started to slip it on me I stopped her. "I'll be too hot with a shirt and a T-shirt on."

I slipped off the T-shirt, mussing my hair, and put on the shirt. Mom fixed my hair with her fingers as I buttoned the shirt and stuck it inside my jeans.

"There," she said, backing off a step to look me over. "That's better. Now you look like my handsome son. You'll knock 'em dead, honey."

"Who cares?" I said. "Do I even want to go to school? Do I want to live in this place?"

"Don't start that again," she said, and went to get her handbag.

The only good part of this miserable morning was that Mom drove me to school. We went through a neighborhood that looked a lot like where we used to live. Lots of neat houses with green lawns in front. Lots of big old trees overhanging the street. Long driveways and garages with basketball hoops on them.

We found the school and then Mom had to drive around the

3

block twice before she found a place to park. The school yard was empty, all the kids already inside. I knew we were really late.

Before we got out of the car, Mom looked into her handbag for something. What she took out was our apartment key and the downstairs door key. She'd tied them both on a loop of white string. "Put this around your neck," she said.

"I'll stick it in my pocket," I said as I took it from her.

"No," she said, "around your neck. That way you won't lose them."

"I won't lose the keys," I said. "I'm not a baby."

"Mark," she said in her hard voice, "around your neck. Puh-lease!"

I put the loop of string around my neck. Mom got out of the car, but I sat there for a moment. She looked at me through the window. "Are you coming or not?"

I got out of the car. We started walking down the street toward the school.

"Put a smile on your face," Mom said. "It's not the end of the world."

I didn't answer her. And I didn't smile either.

"You're not going to start crying, are you?" she asked.

I shook my head.

"Buck up, Mark," she said. "It's the start of a brand-new day. A new job for me and a new school for you. We're right at the beginning of a new life."

"What if I liked the old life better?" I asked.

Mom sighed. "There's nothing I can do about that," she said. "It kind of got decided for us. And the sooner you accept that fact, the better off you'll be."

I kept my mouth shut. Mostly because there was nothing to say that I hadn't said a thousand times before. There was nothing to think about that I hadn't puzzled over and over again for half a year now. And thinking about it only made me madder and sadder.

The keys were bouncing against me as we walked. I pulled up the string and slipped them under my shirt where they wouldn't show. As I did that, I felt a little shiver go through me.

The keys felt cold as they touched my heart.

2
SCHOOL DAZE

I hated the school the minute we walked inside.

The school I'd gone to before had a grassy lawn around it and lots of trees. It was sunny inside and was built all on one floor. There was a play yard in the center of it for the kindergarten kids.

This stupid school was three stories high and dark inside. It was made of sooty brick and looked like it was built a hundred years ago.

We waited on a bench in the office for a while. Then a lady led us into the principal's office. His name was Mr. Guma and he had thick eyebrows and ears that stuck out from his head. He wasn't happy to see Mom and me.

"But you have nothing to show that you live in this school district," he said to Mom.

"We just moved here," Mom said back to him, "only last week."

"Don't you have a telephone bill, or a utility bill?"

"The telephone was installed the day we moved in, on Friday," said Mom. "I gave them a check for the security deposit."

"No receipt?"

"The check is my receipt," said Mom, "when I get it back."

Mr. Guma didn't like that. He and Mom argued back and forth. I just sat like a lump in a chair by Mr. Guma's desk, not paying attention. I thought maybe Mr. Guma wouldn't let me into the school and I'd have to go back to my old school . . . and I'd see all my friends again. But even as I daydreamed, I knew in my heart it wasn't going to happen.

I'd been getting very good at daydreaming lately. I usually imagined myself back in our house, or in the kitchen with Dad and Mom.

Finally, Mom found a deposit receipt from our new apartment in her handbag. That seemed to make Mr. Guma happy. Mom handed him the records she'd brought from my old school and he gave her some forms and papers to fill out.

Mr. Guma looked over my records and smiled at me. "You've done pretty well, Mark," he said, "—really good grades."

I shrugged.

"What happened last term . . . in fifth grade?" he asked me. "Your grades fell way off."

Before I could answer, Mom spoke up. "Trouble at home," she said. "Mark's a really bright student."

Mr. Guma filled out a card and handed it to Mom. "I'm putting you in Mr. Pangalos's class," he said to me. "He's very nice. You'll like him, Mark."

In the outer office a woman took the card from Mom and

said she would walk me to my classroom. As we went out into the hall Mom leaned down to me. "Do you want me to go with you to your class and speak to your teacher?"

I shook my head. That was the last thing in the world I wanted.

Mom glanced at her wristwatch and made a face. "A good thing I told them I'd be late," she said, "because now I really am. Do you have money for lunch?"

"Yes."

"And you know how to get home from school?"

"I think so."

"You just walk back down the same street we drove up on," she said.

"Right." I nodded.

"And if you're not sure, ask a kid walking your way. Or ask the crossing guard. Nobody else."

"Okay."

"And then go right upstairs to the apartment and double-lock the door. Don't let anyone else in, Mark, right?"

"Right."

"And I'll be home at six o'clock, okay?"

"Okay."

Mom looked at me for a moment. "Did we forget anything?"

Only then did I remember. "Yeah . . . my knapsack. With my pens and my notebook inside." I got a really bad feeling right then, and for a second I thought I might cry.

Mom leaned down to kiss me, then turned her head at the last second and just brushed me with her cheek. "Hang in," she said, "It's only the first day." Then she turned and walked away down the hall, and it was the worst I'd felt so far.

The office lady took me up a flight of dark stairs to the second floor. Then we went down the hall to room 233. When we walked into the room the teacher was writing things on the blackboard. "A new arrival," said the office lady.

She handed my card to the teacher. "Hi," he said to me, "I'm Mr. Pangalos." Then he checked my card. "Mark Baker," he said. "Is that you?"

I started to say yes but my throat closed up, so I just nodded.

Mr. Pangalos turned to the class. "Kids, we have a newcomer to our school and to our class. This is Mark Baker. Please make him feel welcome." Mr. Pangalos started clapping his hands and most of the kids did the same while they looked me over. My cheeks turned hot and I felt like a fool.

Mr. Pangalos looked around the room while the kids stared at me. I saw a boy in the middle of the room whisper something to the kid next to him, and then both of them snickered.

I knew they were laughing at me.

I followed Mr. Pangalos as he walked along the side of the room near the windows. He walked all the way to the back of the room, to the very last seat in the corner. Back in my old school that's where the dummies sat. "Let this be your seat for now," he said to me. "And, Mark, please copy down all the information I'm putting on the board."

"Well," I said before I sat down, "I don't have a notebook or a pen."

Mr. Pangalos gave me a questioning look.

"Forgot my knapsack," I mumbled, feeling like an idiot.

9

THE SQUEAKY WHEEL

Mr. Pangalos's mouth scrunched up as he looked around the class. "Libby," he said to a girl a few seats away, "could you please lend Mark a pen and some paper?"

He was speaking to a girl with short hair and thick eyebrows. She opened the loose-leaf book she had on her desk and slipped out two sheets of paper. Then she reached down for her knapsack and found a ballpoint pen inside.

Mr. Pangalos went back to the front of the room and began writing more stuff on the blackboard.

Libby walked over to my desk and handed me the paper and pen. I said thanks.

"You can keep the pen," she said.

I said thanks again.

A boy two seats in front of me whispered, "Libby Klein, clinging vine," and the two boys who'd laughed at me before laughed again.

Libby stuck her tongue out at the boy. "You're a birdbrain, Billy Alston," she said to him under her breath, then she went back to her seat.

I started copying all the things Mr. Pangalos was putting on the board. I felt alone and stupid and out of place. I didn't want to be here.

If I were back in my old school I'd be sitting down front. If I were there I'd be someplace near my friends, Brett and Justin. If this were my old class I'd know everyone in it.

> And when ifs and buts
> become candy and nuts,
> we'll all have a Merry Christmas.

It was a long morning.

3

LUNCH BUNCH

What a disgusting lunchroom!

The lunchroom in my old school was big and bright and had windows that went from floor to ceiling. It was a multipurpose room that was also the gym. This stupid school's lunchroom was down in the basement. It was dark and the tables were all crowded together.

Also, the lunch line was a zillion miles long. And slow as a limpy snail. I inched along behind some of the kids in my class. I didn't know anyone, of course, so I just watched as they talked and kidded around and I felt left out. About half the kids had brought lunch from home and they were already sitting at the tables and eating. Finally I got to where the trays and utensils were.

The lunch was orange-colored macaroni, salad, bread, and canned pears. I paid for it, took a milk, and started looking around for a place to sit. I spotted a seat open and headed for it. But when I put my tray down on the table Billy Alston said, "I'm saving this seat for Steve Mayer."

I picked up my tray again and looked around. I saw Libby Klein sitting with some kids from our class, but there wasn't an empty seat at that table. I walked away and found a spot at a table where no one looked familiar.

Nobody even looked at me. Everyone was busy talking and eating. I ate some of the macaroni and all of the bread, poked at the pears, and drank my milk. I really missed Brett and Justin right then. We always sat together at lunch, and if there was time afterward we'd go outside and throw a ball around.

It was a poky, slow afternoon and I was very glad when school was over. There was the usual hubbub outside with kids yelling and running every which way. Mothers of the little kids were standing around waiting for them. A few school buses and a lot of cars were lined up at the curb.

I saw Libby Klein walking with some kids and I waved at her. She smiled and I started walking to catch up with her, but she and her friends turned the wrong way at the corner. I was going the opposite way.

I walked back toward Beverly Road, through the neighborhood I'd seen from the car this morning. It still reminded me of where I used to live. On the next street I passed a house almost exactly like ours. It was two stories high and the shingles were painted white, like ours, and all the windows had black wooden shutters. There was a long porch in front, too, just like where Mom and Dad would sit having coffee after dinner while I ran around catching fireflies.

I missed my dad. I really and truly missed him, and it was getting me more worried every day.

We hadn't been alone together for almost a month. And the last time I'd spoken to him on the telephone was a week ago. I left messages for him, saying I'd called, but he hardly ever called me back. He and Mom were getting divorced. They said they didn't love each other anymore.

But it looked like Dad was divorcing me too. And I loved him more than ever.

It took about ten minutes to get to Beverly Road. On the last street I saw a kid walking ahead of me who was in my class. I hurried along and caught up with him. "Hey," I said when I got alongside of him, "aren't you in Mr. Pangalos's class?"

He looked at me through his black-rimmed eyeglasses. He was a Chinese kid, skinny and just a touch taller than me. "You're the new kid," he said to me. "What's your name again?"

"Mark Baker."

"I'm Joe Chang," he said. "Do you live around here?"

"Yep. In the apartment house across from the A & P."

"Number two ten."

"Right."

"I know that building," Joe said. "When did you move in?"

"Last Friday."

"Wow," said Joe, "you really are new."

We started walking again and I asked Joe what kind of teacher Mr. Pangalos was. "Fair," he said, "but strict. You better do the work you're supposed to do."

"Right."

"Dot all the *i*'s and cross all the *t*'s," he said. "And don't fool around too much in class."

By this time we'd reached Beverly Road. I had to turn left here and I hoped Joe was going my way. "Nope," he said, "I live two blocks the other way."

"See you," I said as we parted company.

I waited for the traffic light to turn green, then crossed the street and walked to my house. The street door was open when I walked in, and there was an old woman in the outer lobby. She gave me a sharp look. "What do you want?" she asked.

"I live here," I said.

The old woman looked me up and down. "Why don't I know you?" she asked. She had two A & P grocery bags on the floor at her feet.

"We just moved in last Friday," I said.

"Is that so?" she said in a suspicious voice.

"Yes."

"Then you can open the inner door for me," she said.

I fished the keys out from under my shirt, found the key for the downstairs door, and turned it in the lock. I opened the door and held it for the woman.

"I guess you live here after all," she said. She began to pick up her packages.

"Can I help you?" I asked as she passed through into the inner lobby.

"I'm right down the hall," she said.

She still looked and sounded suspicious of me. When I passed by the elevator and went up the stairs she stood and watched me until I made the first turn in the staircase.

The second floor hallway was dark. I used my other key,

14

opened our apartment door, and went inside. Then I double-locked the door behind me, just like Mom said. I started to say "I'm home," but stopped the words on my lips.

Who was there to hear them?

4

THE SECOND-WORST DAY

The first thing I did was turn on the light in the foyer. Then I went to the kitchen and turned the light on in there, then the big lamp in the living room. I know that makes me sound like I was a scared baby, but it looked very dark inside the apartment.

Back in the kitchen I took a glass of milk and two cookies. I sat at the table and chewed the cookies slowly, taking sips of milk in between and looking out the small window over the sink. That window faced the courtyard and all I could see was a telephone pole and the windows on the other side of the building.

If you want to know the truth, I really felt like crying. Make that actually bawling my head off. But what good would that do? Things were exactly the way they were. Nothing was going to change. My dad and all my friends were in another town. Some family I didn't know was probably moving into our old house and a stranger was going to sleep in my old room.

My old life was over, face it. I kept thinking that, turning it around and around in my head.

I'd never live in that great house again.

My dad would never live with me and Mom again.

I'd never see my old friends again.

I opened my mouth and let out a yell: *BLLLAAAAAAAAH-HHHHH!!!*

Then I banged my fist down so hard on the table, the empty milk glass bounced up and fell over on its side. Then I thought of every curse word I knew and said them out loud.

It didn't make me feel any better.

I walked into the living room and stared out the front window. A bus passed by down below. I could see a bearded man in Mostly Books talking on the telephone. A sign in the window of the A & P said there was a special on chicken legs and thighs.

> Legs and thighs,
> begs and sighs,
> cries and cries
> until he dies. . . .

I didn't want to think about my old life, but I couldn't help it. Last year Mom would have been home with me on the first day of school. I'd be sitting in our big kitchen right now, telling her all about what happened in school. After that I'd probably run across the driveway to Brett's house and we'd get out the basketball and shoot some hoops. Then Justin would come along and we'd play horse or five-three-one. I could see

Brett so clearly in my mind, shooting from the corner near the rosebush. He hardly ever missed that shot.

That's when I thought of calling Brett on the telephone. I went to the wall phone in the kitchen and dialed his number. I heard Mrs. Sommers pick up and say hello. "Hi," I said, "it's me, Mark. Can I talk to Brett?"

"Mark!" Mrs. Sommers exclaimed. "How are you? How's your mom?"

"Fine," I said. "Is Brett home?"

"Oh, Mark," she said, "no, he's not. He and Justin went off to buy school supplies."

"Well," I said, "tell him I called."

Mrs. Sommers chattered on for a while, but I was barely listening. I was thinking about Brett and Justin. I knew exactly where they were, at the Bonton Store on Main Street. And if I weren't here in this dark apartment I'd be with them.

I felt pretty low when I hung up the telephone.

I walked into the living room and switched on the TV. I didn't care what was on. I just wanted to sit in the corner of the couch and let the TV wash all thought out of my brain.

Judge Wapner was in his court, looking fuzzy because the TV was not yet hooked up to the master antenna on the roof. Two goofy-looking people were arguing about a poodle that had been given a haircut.

"It was not the cut I told him to give my dog," said this fat lady in pink pants.

"Wrong," said the skinny man with a mustache. "It was exactly the cut we agreed on."

"Your honor," said the fat lady, "he gave me back a dog that was completely bald."

I started thinking about last Friday, the second-worst day of my life. It was the day the moving men came to our house and we moved out.

Mom and I had spent weeks and weeks packing things into cartons. And throwing away things we wouldn't need and didn't have room for in our apartment. In the morning Mom went off for a few hours to her secretary course. She was studying typing and shorthand and how to run a computer. Dad was paying for it so Mom could find a good job and begin to support herself.

Mom and I got on each other's nerves a lot. I hung out with Brett as much as I could. Then he and his family went away to their place on Arrowhead Lake. I spent time with Justin after that.

It was a long, lonely, terrible, and rotten summer. The house began to look very weird. Mom took the pictures off the walls and wrapped them for moving. We had a tag sale one weekend and sold lots of things from the house and most of what was in the garage. There were empty places where furniture had been and bright spots on the walls where pictures were missing.

We spent a lot of time up in the attic, making piles of stuff to save and piles to throw away. A lot of my old toys were up there and I fought with Mom over them. She wanted to chuck them all out. I wanted to save most of them. I managed to save my baseball card collection, but Mom threw away my Nok-Hockey game because I didn't play with it anymore.

Then we had a big fight over a little xylophone I got for my fifth birthday. I don't know why I wanted it so much; I hadn't touched it in years. But I remembered how I used to love hitting the little metal strips and making silly music. I managed to save it, but a lot of other stuff I wanted went into the trash.

Near the end of August, Dad came by for an afternoon. He and Mom divided some household things between them. And then they started another one of their fights.

I never got used to their fighting, even though I'd seen and heard it a lot. It always made me feel closed up inside, no matter how much I told myself to ignore it.

I listened to them yelling at each other about certain books, record albums, and pictures. They sounded like me and Mom arguing about my old toys, only they were louder and nastier. Finally I couldn't stand it anymore. I got my basketball and went outside to shoot some hoops and dribble around.

Even outside in the driveway I could hear them yelling. I dribbled left, thump-thumping the ball on the asphalt. "If you hadn't!" Mom yelled. *Thump-thump-thump.* "Sure," yelled Dad, "blame it on me like you always do!" *Thump-thump.*

I dribbled away down the driveway toward the street, and in between thumps I still heard the sound of their angry voices. I started dribbling down the block on the sidewalk, then turned the corner. I went around the block and back again, setting a record for dribbling time away and not hearing what scared me so much.

The last few days before the moving men came were the worst. Piles of packed cartons were everywhere. All of our dishes and pots were packed, except for a few old plates. Mom stopped cooking. We ate a lot of sandwiches and take-out food.

And then Mom and I had our last fight, about my bicycle. "There's no place to keep it in our apartment," Mom kept saying.

"But I want it! It's mine."

I lost that argument, like I lost most of the others. And I had to leave my beautiful blue ten-speed bike in Brett's garage until we figured out what to do with it.

That was the end of my hoping that Mom and Dad would change their minds, that we wouldn't move away after all. Leaving my bike behind was the last and final proof that life as I knew it was over, forever and ever.

That last night in my old house I cried myself to sleep. I really hated both Mom and Dad for doing this to me. I wanted to yell at both of them. I wanted to grab and shake them, to hit them with my fists.

And now, sitting in the living room, watching stupid Judge Wapner, my eyes filled with tears.

Stop it, you big baby, I told myself. *Are you going to spend the rest of your life crying?*

I went into the kitchen and stared at the wall phone on the side of the cabinets. It was after five o'clock, my dad could be home by now if he quit early. I dialed his number, waited through three rings, then his voice came on.

It was his phone-answering machine.

"Hi, this is Bill Baker. Sorry I'm not home right now. But if you leave a message for me right after you hear the beep, I'll get back to you as quick as I can. . . ."

I waited for the beep. Then I left my message. "It's me, Dad . . . Mark. And I—I just wanted to say I miss you a lot."

21

THE SQUEAKY WHEEL

I hung up the phone and stared at the wall, wanting to cry again. I don't know why, but I began to bop my head against the cabinet. Not hard, just enough to make a little sound. *Bop . . . bop . . . bop.*

5
TOUGH NOOGIES

I got scared when I heard a key in the lock of the door, but it was Mom. She came in smiling and she had a package in her hands. "Chinese take-out," she said. "Egg drop soup, spareribs, and chow mein. All your favorites." She put the package down and grabbed me in a big hug. Then she mussed my hair with her hand and gave me a kiss on the cheek.

"What a day I had!" she said, squeezing me again. "How was yours, honey?"

"Fine," I lied. Mom put the soup into a pot on the stove, then went to her bedroom to change clothes. When she came back she put the ribs and the chow mein into the microwave oven and poured Cokes for both of us. "I want to hear all about your day," she said as we sat down at the table. "How is Mr. What's-his-face?"

"Pangalos."

"Is he nice?"

"He's okay."

"How about the kids?"

"They're okay too. I guess. Hardly anyone talked to me."

"You're the new kid, Mark," she said. "It's natural."

"Not even at lunch."

"Don't worry, you'll make lots of friends. But it's going to take a while." She got up to put a tiny light under the soup pot on the stove. "Sorry about forgetting your knapsack this morning. We ran out of here this morning like a cattle stampede."

"I borrowed a pen and paper from someone."

"Good. And how's the new school?"

"It's not new," I said. "It's a hundred years old and rotten."

"Maybe it's not that old."

"It's nowhere near as nice as my old school. And the lunchroom is down in the basement and very crowded. I want to start taking lunch from home."

"You will. As soon as I get a little more organized."

"When's that going to be?" I asked.

"Soon."

Mom kept asking questions and I kept answering, until the soup was warm. While Mom put our soup into two bowls and opened the package of crispy noodles, I set the table. It was a good thing I'd helped unload the moving cartons, because I knew where everything was. I put two place mats on the table, paper napkins, soup spoons, and forks.

Mom turned the microwave on, then brought our soup to the table. "The big test," she said as she was about to taste the soup. "Now we find out if the Jade Garden can cook as well as our old Chinese restaurant."

"I'll bet it's awful," I said.

24

"Give it a fair chance," Mom said.

We both started eating, with me chomping on Chinese noodles. After a few minutes we decided that the soup was good. And so were the spareribs and chow mein, when Mom brought them to the table.

"The Jade Garden's really good," Mom said, "and I'm glad. Because we're going to be eating Chinese take-out, Kentucky fried, and pizza for a while. Until I get my head on straight around here."

I must have had a funny look on my face when she said that. Because she said, "Don't start, Mark, okay? I can't face the dirty looks and suffering glances tonight. Not after the day I had."

"I didn't say one word, did I?"

"You don't have to," she said. "I can read your face like a book. I know how rough all this has been on you, but it hasn't exactly been a picnic for me either."

I didn't answer her. I got up from the table and cleared our plates to the sink. Mom poured a glass of milk for me and began making coffee for herself.

The silence between us went on for a while. Mom sat down at the table with her coffee. "Well, Joan," she said out loud, "how was your first day of work?"

"Oh, fine," she answered herself, "considering you haven't worked in twelve years and the computer system you have to learn is as complicated as a Chinese puzzle. Other than that it went all right, except that my boss, Mr. Harrington, was very annoyed that I waltzed into the office after ten o'clock, even though he'd said I could come in late today. But the other people I'll be working with seem nice so far. So I guess, over-all, it's going to be okay."

I felt embarrassed by Mom talking to herself. I sipped my milk.

"Can you try to be just a tiny bit interested, Mark?" she said. She reached across the table and took my hand. "Like it or not, kiddo, we're in this together."

"I don't like it," I said.

"Oh, yes," she said, "you've made that abundantly clear."

"I hate it," I said. "I hate this apartment and I hate my new school and I'll probably never have another friend again."

"What am I going to do with you, Mark?" she asked, sigh-ing. She squeezed my hand and then I took it away. "You're very angry with your dad and me, aren't you?" she asked.

I nodded my head.

"Yeah, right," she said, the corners of her mouth turning down. "Please, Mark, remember that we both love you very much . . . and we'll never stop loving you."

"But you don't love me enough to get back together," I said. "Or move back to our old house."

"No," said Mom. "That's over."

"So what good is it that you love me?" I said, my voice rising a little. "I want to be back in our house and go to my old school and still have all my friends."

"Mark . . ."

"And I want Dad to live with us again."

Mom took a sip of her coffee and looked at me over her cup. "Sweetie," she said, "we've gone over this a hundred times or more. Nothing's going to change. You have to accept it."

"And what if I don't want to?"

She shrugged. "Then it's just tough noogies, kiddo."

"What in the world is *noogies*?" I asked.

A smile came on Mom's face and she giggled. "Something we said when I was a girl. It sort of means . . . things aren't going to change. It's just tough."

I took my milk glass and went over to the sink, turning my back on Mom. Then I began rinsing off the dishes.

"Leave them," Mom said. "I'll clean up."

I shut off the water and dried my hands on a dish towel. Then I started going off to my room.

"Mark," Mom called after me, "will you give me a break?"

I didn't answer, but here's what I almost said: "Tough noogies, Mom."

6

$\mathcal{M}$EET PHIL STEINKRAUS

The lunch line was just as long and slow on my second day in school.

When I got to the end of the line with my tray, I looked around for a place to sit down. It was just like yesterday, all the tables were crowded. I started walking, looking for a spot. In the far corner of the room I saw a table with just one boy sitting at it. I headed that way.

The kid sitting at the table was big. No, better make that huge. He was wearing a T-shirt that said PROPERTY OF THE U.S. ARMY on it. The sleeves of the T-shirt were rolled up and I could see that the kid had these really bulging muscles in his arms.

I put my tray on the table right across from him and started to sit down. The kid stared at me from under thick black eyebrows that met in the center of his forehead. "Hey," he said in a deep, growly voice, "did I say you could sit down here?"

"Nope."

"Then beat it."

I thought about that for a millisecond, then I sat down.

"Maybe you're hard of hearing," the big kid said. "Scram!"

I looked him straight in the eye and took a bite of my food. "I'm hungry," I said. "Besides, it's a free country, last time I heard."

The kid shook his head and smiled at me in a funny way. He had about a zillion pointy teeth in his mouth and his smile reminded me of something. A wolf.

"You just made a big mistake, pal," he said.

I ignored that remark and began opening my carton of milk.

"This afternoon, after school," he said, "I'm going to hand your head to you."

I got a sting of scaredness in my stomach when he said that, but I tried not to let it show. I took another bite of my food and stared back at the big kid.

I have to tell you I was in a bad mood right then. I flat did not care what happened to me. I mean, I was really steamed at the school and the kids in it and my mom and dad and everything under creation. And if this big pile of eyebrows, pointy teeth, and muscles wanted to fight me right there in the lunchroom, that was okay by me.

"What's your name, stupid?" asked the kid.

"Mark Baker," I said. "What's your name, stupid?"

The kid's coal-black eyes opened wide in surprise. "You got to be the dumbest kid in school," he said. "Or else you're new around here."

"I'm new."

"Because nobody—not even teachers—can get away with talking to me like that."

I took another bite of my pizza and chewed on it. "Kind of looks like nobody wants to talk to you anyway," I said. "Or wants to sit anywhere near you."

"That's the way I want it," he said.

I lifted my nose and made a sniffing noise. "You don't smell too bad," I said, "so it can't be that."

The kid shook his crew-cut head, like he couldn't believe I'd said that. "You just keep talking like that and I'll have to rip your lips off."

"You never told me your name."

"Phil Steinkraus. And don't you forget it."

"How could I ever forget a name like Phil Steinkraus!"

"Listen, Mr. Mark the Moron," he said. "I want you to meet me in the yard after school so I can personally punch your lights out."

"Wow!" I said, as if I were impressed. "That's the best invitation I've had all day. Golly gee, that's sure nice of you. If I had my notebook with me I'd write it down. 'Meet Phil Steinkraus in yard after school. Reason: to get lights punched out.' Sure sounds great to me."

Phil Steinkraus kept staring at me like he couldn't figure me out. "What grade are you in?"

"Sixth. How about you?"

"Sixth," he said. "One more time."

"Were you left back?"

"You could say that. I call it dee-tained and ree-tained."

"I get it," I said. "Everybody in sixth likes you so much, they just want to keep you around for another year. Is that about it?"

Phil Steinkraus's mouth opened in a pointy-toothed grin

and then he made this "heh-heh" sound deep down in his throat. It sounded really weird, but it had to be the way he laughed. "You are a funny kid," he said. "Heh-heh, heh-heh."

"That's me."

"Whose class are you in?"

"Mr. Pangalos."

"Old Pangle himself, huh?"

"Is that what they call him?"

"Yeah. I call him Mr. Pangle-till-you-strangle."

"Very poetic," I said. "How is he?"

"Medium. You're really lucky you didn't get Miss DeBoer, like me. That woman won't even let me turn around without she's all over my case."

"She's tough, huh?"

"Old Miss Boring is the worst," he said.

"Then why don't you meet her out in the yard and punch her lights out?" I said.

"Heh-heh, heh-heh."

"You could rip her lips off too," I said. "Do a really good job."

"Heh-heh, heh-heh." Phil Steinkraus was really laughing hard now, showing me all his pointy teeth. "You are a riot, pal," he said. Then he reached a thick arm across the table and punched me on the shoulder. Lightly, thank heaven. "Mark Baker," he said, "you and me, we're gonna have a great time this year."

7
ONE-DOLLAR FRIEND

That afternoon we got our textbooks to take home, and our first homework.

We had an election for class officers too. There were two kids running for president. One was Libby Klein, who'd loaned me a pen and paper. The other was Steve Mayer. He was the one I'd thought was making remarks and laughing at me. No way I was going to vote for him.

It wasn't even close. Libby won by a landslide, and a boy, Ned Robbins, was elected vice-president. A pretty girl with long brown hair, Joyce Appleman, became class secretary.

Finally, the last bell rang and school was over for the day. At the curb outside the school Phil Steinkraus was holding a knapsack high over his head. A small boy was jumping up and down, trying to get the knapsack back. Phil spotted me and yelled, "Hey, Marky! Over here!" Then he whirled the knapsack around his head a few times and let it fly. The small boy ran down the street after it.

"Which way are you walking?" Phil asked me.

I told him and we started walking away from the school together. We crossed the street and went about half a block before Phil spoke. "It's rotten, ain't it?"

"What's rotten?"

"Everything," he said. "The school, the teachers, the classes —the whole mess."

"Why were you ragging the little kid?" I asked.

Phil shrugged. "No reason. I just felt like it."

"Anybody ever do that to you?"

"Are you nuts?" he said. "Nobody messes with me, boy. I'm too big, too tough, and too ugly. I'm a lean, mean fighting machine."

"And a poet too," I said.

The wolf grin came onto Phil's face. "You got that right, Marky."

"Mark," I said. "Nobody ever calls me Marky."

"Okay, Marky," Phil said, punching me lightly on the shoulder.

We walked along for a while, not saying much. It was a bright day and the sun came through the leafy trees overhead and spotted the sidewalk with light and shadow.

"Where do I buy school supplies?" I asked.

"Dealtown. It's right on Beverly Road."

"Wouldn't you know, the minute we get our books they give us homework too. I always wish they'd hold off homework for a while."

Phil laughed. "I remember homework," he said. "As if it ain't horrible enough in school, they make you suffer at home too. I don't even write down what the homework's supposed to be anymore."

I looked at Phil, not believing what I'd heard. "You don't do homework?"

"Nah."

"How do you get away with that?"

"I always say I forgot and left it home."

I didn't believe that. "But after a while they have to stop letting you get away with it, right?"

Phil Steinkraus made a weird face. "Ask me no questions and I'll tell you no lies," he said.

We got to Beverly Road and turned away from my house. There were lots of shops and stores on the street and a few apartment buildings like mine.

"You got money on you?" Phil asked.

I nodded.

"Can you lend me ten dollars?"

"Not that much," I said.

"How much you got?"

"Enough to buy school supplies," I said.

"Then loan me five bucks," Phil said, and he stuck out his hand.

I felt really funny about that. I didn't know Phil Steinkraus too well. And what I did know about him wasn't all that great. On the other hand, nobody else in school seemed to know I was alive.

I had fifteen dollars in my pocket, a ten-dollar bill with five singles wrapped around it. I reached into my pocket carefully and came up with the outside dollar bill. "Here's a dollar," I said. I held it out toward Phil but he wouldn't touch it.

34

"You just failed the test," he said.

"What test?"

"Now I know just what you are, Marky boy," said Phil. "You're nothing but another one-dollar friend."

"What do you mean?"

"Forget about it," he said.

"Tell me."

"Who knows?" He shrugged. "Maybe sometime I will. If we stay friends long enough. Which I doubt."

Dealtown was a few doors down the street. I really wanted to know what Phil meant by a "one-dollar friend," but I didn't insist he tell me. I had already figured out that Phil wasn't a kid you insisted to very much.

Phil opened the door and we walked into the store. Up front there was a counter with a cash register on it. The man behind the counter came in. "You!" he said in a loud voice, and he pointed his finger at Phil. "You just hold it right there."

"Howdy doody, Mister Atkins," said Phil Steinkraus with a grin.

Mr. Atkins came running out from behind the counter. "Get out of here!" he said, jerking his thumb at the door. "I told you never to set foot in here again, Steinkraus."

"Hey," said Phil, "is this a free country, or what?"

"Out!" said Mr. Atkins.

"Awright," said Phil, "don't have a heart attack. I just brought my friend Marky in to buy school supplies."

Mr. Atkins stepped right in front of us so we couldn't get past him. "Get out or I'll throw you out," he growled at Phil. "And if you don't like it, call a cop. Now, scram!"

Phil's lip curled back and he muttered a curse word loud enough to hear. Then he turned for the door.

I was shocked, to tell the truth. I didn't know what to do.

Phil opened the door. "Looks like I gotta go, Marky," he said. "See ya round."

Mr. Atkins stood in front of me and looked me over. "Do I know you?"

"No."

"Is that mug your friend?"

I hesitated for just a second, then nodded.

"Better give me your knapsack, son," he said.

"What for?"

"So you don't put things in it accidentally on purpose," he said. "Things you don't pay for."

"Wait a minute," I said, getting mad. "I never stole anything in my life. And I have money to pay for everything I need."

"Good," said Mr. Atkins. "Then you won't mind letting me hold your knapsack while you shop."

I slipped my knapsack off and handed it to him. I felt very insulted, but I didn't know what to do about it. "I am not a crook," I said.

"Glad to hear it," he said. "But your pal Steinkraus sure is."

I picked up a little shopping basket and walked away from the front of the store. I didn't like Mr. Atkins, but his store was neat. It had lots of toys as well as school supplies. I walked along, looking over the toys, and calming down. As I got to the back of the store I heard some kids yelling in the next aisle. I peeked around the corner to see what was going on and I was amazed.

There were a bunch of kids from my class and two of them were having a fight on the floor!

Michael Marder was on top of Billy Alston and they were wrestling and trying to punch each other. Steve Mayer was smiling, standing behind Libby Klein and Ned Robbins.

"Michael, quit it!" Libby said.

Then Mr. Atkins came running and broke up the wrestling match. He grabbed Billy Alston and marched him away, then Steve Mayer walked after them. Michael Marder got up from the floor holding a hand over his eye.

"What happened?" I asked Libby.

She just shrugged, but Ned Robbins said it was a disagreement.

"Looks like more than that to me," I said.

"It's a long story," Libby said. "And a stupid one."

Pretty soon they all went up to the front of the store, paid for their purchases, and left. I kept shopping and had my basket almost full. Then I took a minute to figure out how much everything cost and ended up putting my extra packs of pens and pencils back on the shelves.

I took my stuff to the front of the store to get checked out. "I owe you a knapsack, don't I?" said Mr. Atkins after I'd paid him. He found it behind the counter and handed it to me.

"I think you owe me an apology too," I said.

"Guess I do at that," he said. He asked my name and I told him. "Well, Mark," he said, "I've caught that Steinkraus kid shoplifting three different times. That's three strikes—you're out—in my book. Is that guy really a friend of yours?"

"I just met him," I said.

"Well, see if you can unmeet him," he said. "That kid is headed for big trouble. Phil Steinkraus is bad news and bad company."

8

DAD'S DAY

Dad had said he'd pick me up at nine o'clock that Sunday morning. I was up at seven, washed, and ready to go a few minutes later. Mom was still sleeping. I took a glass of milk and sat on the arm of the couch in the living room, looking out the window and waiting for Dad.

The A & P was open and they'd changed the signs in the window. There was a special on chuck roast, which sounded like a piece of meat you could actually greet. "Hi, I'm Chuck Roast. And this is my brother, Pot."

Nine o'clock went by and I began to get nervous. Maybe Dad wasn't going to show up like he'd said. Mom was making coffee in the kitchen and I sat with her, looking at the clock every few minutes. "Same old dependable Dad," she said, but I didn't answer.

At ten minutes after ten the downstairs buzzer rang. I ran over and rang back so Dad could get in the inner door downstairs. Then I opened the apartment door and waited for him.

When he came up the stairs I ran into the hall and jumped into his arms.

"Hey, Mark," he said, holding me in a bear hug, "how's my boy?"

I didn't say anything, I just held on to him real tight, feeling his big arms around me, smelling his special smell of tobacco, washed shirt, and shaving lotion.

Mom came to the door, holding her coffee cup. "Hello, Bill," she said. "You're late."

"Not too much," said Dad, putting me down.

"Over an hour," Mom said.

"I didn't know you were timing me," Dad said. "Has he had breakfast yet?"

"Just some milk," I said.

"Good," said Dad, "then we can get breakfast on the road." He took a few steps into the foyer and looked around. "Not bad," he said to Mom. "How are you guys getting on?"

"Just fine," said Mom. Her mouth was set in the skinny smile she puts on when she's mad. "How's your apartment?"

"Tiny," Dad said. "I'm just about settling in. How's your job?"

"Not too bad," Mom replied. "How's business?"

"Could be better."

My parents looked at each other for a long moment, not saying anything. I don't know why, but I expected them to start yelling at each other.

"Well," Dad said to me, "are you ready to roam?"

I nodded.

"Then let's hit the road, toad," he said.

"What time will you have him back?" asked Mom.

Dad shrugged. "Six, seven o'clock."

"Before dinner, or afterward?"

Dad ruffled my hair with his hand. "Who knows?" he said. "If we're having fun I'll keep him through dinner."

"Oh, no," said Mom, "you're not hanging me up like you always do. Tell me right now if I have to have dinner for him or not."

"Fine," said Dad, "I'll have him back by six o'clock, then. He has school tomorrow and I have to work."

"Not to mention you probably have plans for tonight," said Mom.

I could feel Dad's hand stiffen on my head, and when I looked up at him his ears were starting to get red. "Now, Joan," he said, "please don't start."

"Me start?" said Mom. "Seems to me you were the one who started everything."

Dad stared at her, his big hands clenching and unclenching. "Let's get out of this place, Mark," he said, then he turned and walked out the door.

"Have a swell time with your father," Mom said as she gave me a peck on the cheek. She didn't sound like she meant it.

My Dad is a big guy, six foot three with lots of muscles. One of his hands is almost as big as my whole head. He's an electrical contractor. He can fix anything with electricity in it, and lots of things without it. Dad always wears jeans or blue workpants and blue work-shirts with his name on the pocket. The lettering on the door of his pickup truck says WILLIAM BAKER, ELECTRICAL CONT. When he and Mom split up, she got to keep the Toyota and he kept the truck.

THE SQUEAKY WHEEL

People always say I look like Dad, but I don't see it. I don't have a big mustache like he does, for one thing. But my nose is like his, short and straight, and we both have gray eyes and hair that's almost blond.

We had breakfast in a Hojo, which Dad likes a lot. It was on a bypass near where we used to live. We sat in a booth that looked out on the road.

Dad always has the breakfast special in a Hojo: pancakes, sausage, hash browns, bacon, two eggs, and coffee. And then Dad orders toast on the side.

I ordered French toast and picked at it while Dad ate everything in sight, including the last piece of my syrupy toast. Seeing Dad and Mom so angry at each other made my appetite go away.

It wasn't always like that. I remember years and years of my life when things were good at home. Mom and Dad and me, we hung close together like a bunch of grapes. My parents kissed a lot back then, and sometimes Dad would make a family hug. He'd wrap me and Mom in his big arms and we all squished together and laughed.

Now Mom and Dad couldn't spend two minutes together without getting mad. Something happened about a year or so ago that just broke everything apart. I think I know what it was, but it's too awful to think about.

They just stopped loving each other. And the fighting started.

"Great breakfast," Dad said. He signaled the waitress and got more coffee for himself. "So," he said to me, "what would you like to do today?"

"Whatever you want," I said. "As long as we're together."

"So we'll just hang out, huh?"

"Sure."

"Fine," said Dad. "There's a ball game on TV today. We could stay at my place and watch it. Or we could try and see a movie."

"Anything you like," I said. I watched him light a cigarette and I had it in mind to ask him some things. Like, why he didn't call me more often on the telephone. Or why I hadn't seen him in more than two weeks. But I didn't want to spoil the good feeling I had. Just being with Dad, even doing nothing special, that made everything all right.

Dad took a sip of his coffee. He looked out on the highway, where cars were zipping by. "Actually," he said, "it might be a good idea for you to meet someone."

"Who?"

"A very nice woman named Trudy. You'll like her, Mark. She's a sweet person."

I didn't want to believe what Dad was saying, but I knew exactly what it meant. My dad had a girlfriend. A stupid, rotten girlfriend named Trudy who was not my mom. My fingers fiddled with the paper napkin in my lap as I thought about it.

It was scary. My dad and Trudy, whoever she was. A new woman to take the place of Mom. I wanted to say something about it, but I couldn't think what. So I sat like a dummy, curling and uncurling the end of the paper napkin in my lap.

"Trudy's fun," Dad said. "She has a great sense of humor."

I nodded at him, unable to speak.

"Your choice," Dad said. "We can go over to her place or not. Whatever you want."

Suddenly tears came to my eyes and began rolling down my cheeks. I covered my face with the paper napkin.

"Oh, Mark," Dad said, like he was disappointed in me. He got out of his side of the booth and slid into mine, then put his arms around me and cradled my head against his shirt. "I know, baby, I know," he said. "It's really tough on you."

"Why'd you have to do it?" I sobbed. "Why?"

Dad didn't answer.

It was all coming back again, all the terrible feelings I'd had on the worst day of my life. That was the day my parents sat me down in the kitchen and told me straight out that they didn't love each other anymore. The next thing they said was that they couldn't go on living together. In that couple of minutes it seemed like my whole world was torn apart.

"But we both love you, Mark," they said next. "We love you very much."

And I remember thinking . . . *That's a lie.* If they loved me so much they wouldn't be splitting up. It wasn't true. The next thing I thought was that there was something wrong I'd done. Maybe I was bad. Maybe the whole thing was my fault.

And after that I started to get really mad at both of them for doing this to me. And I still felt that way: bad and mad and scared all mixed up in a terrible tangle I couldn't understand.

Dad gave me his hankie and I rubbed my eyes with it, then blew my nose. "Why'd you do it?" I asked. "Why'd you have to sell our house and move away?"

"Mark, we told you all that. More than once."

"Tell me again. Maybe I'm stupid and I can't understand."

Dad pulled his coffee cup across the table. He took a small

sip. "You're not stupid. You're very smart, in fact, and you know you are."

"But not smart enough to keep you and Mom together," I said.

Dad sighed and made an annoyed face. "It's nothing to do with you."

Another lie, is what I thought. It had everything to do with me. Everything in my whole life. But I didn't say it.

"It's between your mom and me," he said. "You're a good son, Mark. The best, from the minute you were born. We loved you then and we love you even more now."

"But not enough to get together again," I said.

"No," he said. "It's not going to happen. And if you keep on thinking it will, you'll just keep beating yourself up."

"I can't help it," I said. "Sometimes when the phone rings I'm sure it's you and you're saying you want to come back, and I call Mom and she picks up the phone and says everything's okay and we should see if we can buy our old house back and live in it again. That's what I think sometimes, Dad."

"Mark," Dad said, "let it go."

"I can't."

"Listen to me," he said, putting his hand over mine. "You've got to let it go. Your Mom and me . . . we just sort of drifted away from each other. Not because of you. In fact, we stayed together for you for a couple of years. Until we plain couldn't do it anymore. We were making each other miserable and unhappy. And life . . ."

Dad rubbed a finger across his mustache.

"Life is supposed to be happy, Mark. There's supposed to be

good things in it. Some fun, some love, some happy feelings. Or else it's too sad and too lonely to get through. A person can't live like that, sad all the time. Do you understand?"

"Yeah"—I nodded—"I know about sad."

"Your mom will find someone else sometime. Some nice man who will make her happy. And maybe I will too. . . ."

"And what about me?"

"It will get better for you, believe me. You'll make new friends in school. You'll have Mom every day and I'll try to see you on Sundays. And telephone during the week, if I remember. You'll see, Mark, all this will pass. Just hang in there and toughen up."

Toughen up? It sounded just like tough noogies. Mom and Dad were going to find people to make them happy. And me? I had to toughen up.

We sat awhile in silence. I watched the cars and trucks going by on the sunny highway outside the window.

"So I guess we'll just spend the day alone, huh?" said Dad.

"I just want to be with you," I said. "Alone."

"Right," said Dad. "Then maybe I'd better go phone Trudy. Tell her not to expect us."

Dad got up from the booth and walked toward the phone booths in the rear of the restaurant. I watched him go, my fingers fiddling with the keys under my shirt.

I knew Dad had wanted me to meet this Trudy person. And I knew I'd disappointed him by saying no.

But as I thought about her, here came the mads again. *Toughen up, Dad.*

9

STEINKRAUS AND COMPANY

Mom had a zillion questions for me when Dad dropped me off that night. Did you have a good time? Did you see Dad's new apartment? Did Dad seem happy? Did he mention someone I don't know?

I felt like she was Judge Wapner and I was in her court.

But I kept my mouth shut about Trudy. Because I knew it was going to hurt Mom the way it was already hurting me.

To change the subject I started asking about my bike that was stored in Brett's garage. I wanted that bike. Riding it was one of the things I loved to do and couldn't anymore.

"There's just no place to keep it, Mark," Mom insisted. "We still have all these unpacked moving cartons and no room to put them."

I had no answer to that. But I still wanted my bike back.

In school the next day I almost made my first friend besides Phil Steinkraus. Her name is Carrie White. She has blond hair and blue eyes and wears some kind of colored stuff around her eyes.

I think she is a bubblehead.

On the way to the auditorium she walked up beside me and introduced herself. "Hi," I said, which was a little funny, because we'd been in the same class for a week now. But we still had to say hi to each each other as if we were strangers from the moon.

"Do you have a girlfriend?" Carrie asked me.

"No."

The boy who'd been in the fight at Dealtown, Michael Marder, was walking beside us. He had a funny-looking eye that was colored maroon, purple, and yellow, probably from getting it punched. When Michael heard Carrie ask me about a girlfriend, he started laughing.

"Do you want a girlfriend?" Carrie asked me.

"I don't know," I said. "I never had one."

"You are amazing," Michael said to Carrie. "Leave the kid alone, will you?"

"Stay out of this, Michael," Carrie said.

Michael made a goony face at her and walked away.

"The thing of it is," said Carrie, "are you going to Libby's birthday party?"

"No," I said, "I wasn't invited."

"You could go with me, if you want," she said. "I could talk to Libby and ask her to invite you. Would you like that?"

I shrugged. "I don't know Libby too well."

"Doesn't matter," Carrie said. "If I told Libby you were my new boyfriend, then she'd invite you."

"Oh," I said.

"So how about it?"

"Is that the deal?" I asked. "I have to become your boy-friend to go to Libby's party?"

"Uh-huh."

"No deal," I said, but then I saw the disappointed look on Carrie's face. "I mean, thanks," I added quickly, "but no thanks. I mean, I would really like to go to Libby's party, but I don't really want to have a girlfriend right now."

Carrie stopped walking and I did too. She looked like she was annoyed with me.

"Let's get this straight, okay?" I said. "If I wanted a girl-friend, which I don't, then maybe I'd pick you. Because except for that blue stuff under your eyebrows you are pretty. But I think a person should get to know another person before they become a girlfriend or a boyfriend, okay?"

"That doesn't matter to me," said Carrie.

"Well, it does to me."

"We could get to know each other *after*," she said.

"I'm sorry," I said, "but the answer is still no."

"Okay," she said.

"Nothing personal," I said. "But I hardly know you or any-one else in the class."

"I understand," Carrie said. "But can I ask you some other time to be my boyfriend?"

"Sure," I said, although I wasn't sure I was sure.

Carrie smiled at me then and walked away, leaving me standing in the hall. I was extremely confused. In about a minute I got invited to be a boyfriend and invited to Libby's party. Now neither was going to happen.

THE SQUEAKY WHEEL

Phil Steinkraus was waiting outside school when classes were over. "Let's go to your house," he said.

"Can't," I said. "My mom won't let me bring anyone home when she's not there."

"So what?"

"So we can't," I said.

"You listen to her?" Phil asked, a smile on his face.

"Yes."

Phil made a kind of horselaugh between his lips. "Then we'll go to my house," he said, and grabbed my arm.

I really didn't want to go with him, but Phil squeezed the muscles in my arm so hard, I'd thought they'd break. "Okay, okay," I said, and he let me go. "But I can't stay long. I have a lot of homework."

"You don't have to do it," said Phil as we started walking.

"Maybe you don't," I said, "but I do."

We started walking in a new direction for me. I kept checking street signs, because I didn't want to get lost on the way home.

"School is stupid," Phil said. "I don't know why I need it."

"Well," I said, "you've got to know how to read and write."

"I can do that. So what?"

"Depends on what you want to do later," I said. "I may be an electrical contractor like my dad. Or maybe I'll want to build houses or something. I'll probably go to college."

"And while you're in college," said Phil, "I'll be getting paid. Four more years and I'll get Mom to sign the paper for me. Then I'm going straight into the army."

"How old are you, anyway?"

"Thirteen. Fourteen in May."

"Wow."

"When I'm seventeen, I'm going airborne."

"You mean . . . jumping out of airplanes?" I couldn't believe anyone would actually want to do that. "Don't you think that's a little dangerous?"

"Only if your parachute won't open," said Phil. "Then it's scary for only a minute or two."

As we walked along, the houses were getting smaller and there were more of them on every street. Phil turned into the yard of one of them. "Home sweet home," he said.

The yard was mostly dirt and just a little grass. On the porch there were some wooden chairs that needed painting. Phil opened the front door and we went inside. I hate to say this, but the place smelled bad. Like cabbage or broccoli or some vegetable Mom cooks once in a while.

"Philly? Is that you?" called a woman's voice.

"My sister's home," Phil said.

I followed him into the kitchen. A very fat young woman wearing a blue apron was standing near the kitchen table.

"This is my big sister, Candy," said Phil. "She goes to beauty school."

"Hi," I said, "I'm Mark."

"Pleased ta meetcha," Candy said. She was chewing gum and she popped it. She had a lot of brown hair piled up way high on her head and she was wearing brown lipstick.

Phil went to the refrigerator and took out two cans of beer. "You want a beer, Marky?" he asked me.

I shook my head.

Phil opened a can of beer and took a big gulp of it. He belched really loud.

"Put the other can away, Philly," said Candy. "You know how Mom is when we finish her beer." *Pop!* went her gum.

"What'd you do in school today?" Phil asked her.

"We're still on fingernails," Candy said. "Sit down at the table." *Pop!* "I got to get some practice."

"Again?" said Phil. "You did my nails yesterday."

"So I'll remove the polish and do them again," she said. Then Candy turned her eyes on me. "Unless your friend wants a manicure."

"I don't think so," I said.

Candy came over and took my hands in hers. She gave each of them a careful look, turning them this way and that. "You really should stop biting your cuticles," she said.

"I don't bite my cuticles," I said.

"They look absolutely horrible," she said. *Pop!* "You must be doing something to 'em."

"Maybe I pick them a little," I admitted.

"More than a little," she said.

"When I'm thinking," I said.

"You must think a lot," said Candy. "But I'm gonna fix 'em up for you real pretty."

"Wait," I said as she started to pull me by my hands. But Candy held on to my hands and led me to the table. She had emery boards and nail polish and other things there.

"Sit down," she said. *Pop!* "I'm not gonna hurt you even one little bit."

I must have had a strange look on my face, because Phil started laughing. "Sit down, Marky," he said. "She needs to practice. You don't want my sis to fail nails, do you?"

I sat down. Candy popped her gum. Then she picked up a small wooden stick and started pushing back my cuticles.

"This is weird," I said.

"Never hurt you," said Candy. She took a tiny pair of scissors and cut off some hanging cuticle parts.

"I never had a manicure before," I said.

"You could use one every couple weeks," Candy said. "Did you know that some of your finest gents get their nails done regular?"

"Like who?" I asked.

"The President," Candy said. "Of the United States. And Frank Perdue." *Pop!* "Lee Iacocca . . . lots of big people."

"Michael Jackson," Phil chimed in. "He has them done all the time."

I kept my eyes on Candy as she rounded the ends of my fingernails with an emery board. She was right, it didn't hurt at all. But when she reached for a bottle of nail polish, I pulled my hands away. "No polish," I said.

"Of course, polish," she said. "It's the finishing touch that means so much." *Pop!*

"No."

"Come on," she said, "I'm only gonna use clear lacquer." She grabbed one of my hands and began.

"Aw," said Phil, "I think you oughta polish them in Blushing Pink or Honeymoon Red."

"That's not funny," said Candy. *Pop!* "I wouldn't do that to a nice kid like Marky."

"Mark," I said. "Don't call me Marky."

I held still while Candy finished putting that clear polish on

---

53

my nails. They ended up looking really shiny and very neat. Extremely weird, yes, but very neat.

Candy told me to hold my fingers still while the polish dried. As I sat there she kept looking at my face, then reached across the table and took my chin in her hand. "Gosh," she said, "you know you got a really pretty face on you? Good cheekbones and a sweet little nose. Deep-set eyes. And very nice lips."

"Hey," said Phil, "I think I'm falling in love with him. Will you marry me, Marky?"

"You know what?" said Candy. "I could practice my makeup technique on your face, Mark. How about it?"

"No way," I said.

"You just sit right there," said Candy, getting up. "I'll get my makeup case and be back in a sec."

That's when I left the Steinkraus house in a hurry.

10

↑N A JADE GARDEN

I was finishing my homework when Mom called. "Is everything okay, Mark?"

"Sure."

"Where were you when I called at four o'clock?"

"Oh. I went to Phil's house for a while. Then I came home."

"I see," said Mom. "I was concerned. I knew you should have been home from school and the phone just rang and rang."

"You shouldn't worry about me so much."

"But I do, honey. That's a mother's job."

"Well, I'm fine. What's for dinner?"

"The age-old question," she said, "and I don't have the least idea. Maybe we'll eat out tonight."

She came through the door at six o'clock on the dot. "What a day," Mom said. "I'm frazzled and famished. How about we go to the Chinese restaurant down Beverly Road?"

"Chinese food again?" I said.

"Why not?" said Mom. "I promise not to order anything hot." I still remembered the Chinese meal we'd had before we moved. Mom got us a chicken dish that was so spicy, my mouth almost caught on fire.

The Jade Garden was a small restaurant only a couple of blocks away. There were booths along the walls and a few big round tables in the back. Mom gave the small, thin woman behind the cash register a big greeting. "Back again, Helen," she said. "Your take-out food was so good, I brought my son back for dinner."

"Nice to see you again," the Chinese woman said.

A waiter in a white jacket and a bow tie came along and led us to a booth. "Helen's a very nice woman," Mom said. "While I waited for our take-out the other night, she told me where to shop in the neighborhood."

We studied our menus for a few minutes, and Mom said I could have spareribs again. I think I could eat them every day. When the waiter came back, Mom ordered our dinner. "So," she said while we waited to be served, "tell me more about this new friend of yours. Phil somebody."

"Steinkraus. I already told you about him."

"He's big, he's tough, and he hates school. That's all I know."

"Well," I said, "he has a big sister, Candy, who goes to beauty school." And then I told Mom about my afternoon visit to Phil's house and showed her my fingernails.

Mom started laughing just as the waiter brought our egg rolls. "Your hands look fabulous," she said.

"Yeah, I guess they do. But no way was I going to let her put makeup and lipstick on my face."

"Quite right," Mom said, grinning. "Is this Phil in your class?"

"Nope."

I have to admit I was very careful about how much I told Mom about Phil Steinkraus. I think I knew in my heart he wasn't the kind of friend you bring home to show your mother. I wasn't even sure he was a real friend either. But he was the only one I had, and I wasn't ready to give him up.

Besides that, I don't think you have to tell mothers everything.

Just then a small girl came walking toward us from the back of the restaurant. She had her hair in two bunches tied up with white ribbons and she carried a tiny kitten in her arms. She stopped in front of our booth and looked at me. "Do you like pussycats?" she asked me.

"Yes," I said.

"Me too," she said with a grin. "Isn't she pretty? Her name is Cookie."

"Hello, Cookie," I said.

The little girl petted the kitten and held it up near her face. "Say hello to the boy," she told Cookie, then she waited for the kitten to speak. After a moment the little girl said, "She can't talk yet. She's only two weeks old, you know."

"Right," I said.

"And how old are you?" asked Mom.

"Four and a little bit."

"And what's your name?"

"Mishi."

"What a pretty name," Mom said.

The little girl shrugged. "Cookie has to go to sleep now,"

she said, then she walked away to the back and went through the swinging door into the kitchen.

I finished eating my egg drop soup. Then I told Mom about Carrie White. She thought I handled her right.

"I hope you make some new friends soon," she said.

"Me too. But you know what? I'm getting used to being in the apartment alone. It's not so scary anymore."

Mom smiled.

"And I don't have to run home from school every day and lock myself in either. I'm not a baby."

"Fine," she said, "but you must call me at work if you're not going to be home. I always want to know where you are and where you're going."

"Or else you'll worry," I said.

"You got it, kiddo."

"When will you stop worrying?" I asked.

Mom thought for a second. "Probably when you're grown up and married and have your own children. And even then I'll most likely still worry about you. I don't think I'll ever stop having you on my mind, even when I'm very old."

"And then I'll worry about you," I said.

Mom liked that, I could see it in her eyes. She reached over and squeezed my hand.

The waiter came back and cleared away our dishes. Then he brought the rest of our food.

While I was chewing on a rib, a kid came in the front door and handed some money to the woman behind the cash register. It was Joe Chang, from my class.

"Don't turn around," I told Mom, "but a kid from my class just walked in."

When Joe looked our way, I waved at him. He came over and stood at the end of our booth. "Hi, Mark," he said.

I introduced Joe to my mom. "What are you doing here?" I asked him.

"This is my family's place," he said.

"Wow, are you lucky!" I said. Joe just stared at me. "You can have egg drop soup any time you want."

"I guess," Joe said. "But what I really like is a hamburger. I don't get that too often."

"Why don't you sit down with us for a minute?" Mom suggested.

"I can't," said Joe. "Mom and Dad don't like me to sit with the customers."

"Who's your mom and dad?" I asked.

"My mom is the lady up front by the cash register," Joe said. "My dad is the chef. He's in the kitchen."

"How about the waiter?" I asked. "Is he family too?"

"Yes"—Joe nodded—"my uncle Han. He came over from Hong Kong a few years ago, so his English isn't too good."

"He sounded fine to me," Mom said. "Is that cute little girl your sister?"

"Yes," said Joe.

"Mishi," said Mom. "Is that a Chinese name?"

"Mishi is her nickname," Joe said. "Her name is Michelle."

"I see," said Mom.

No one spoke for a moment, then Joe said he'd better get back to the kitchen.

"Just a minute," Mom said. "Why don't you two boys walk to school together tomorrow? Mark could use a new friend, Joe. He's very lonely."

"Oh, Mom!" I said, feeling my cheeks get warm. "I'm sure that Joe has a million friends."

"You can never have enough friends," Mom said. "How about it, Joe?"

Joe shrugged, and I think he looked as embarrassed as I felt. "Okay," he said. "Eight o'clock. I'll meet you on your corner."

"Okay," I said.

Joe turned away and walked to the back of the restaurant. As soon as he was out of earshot, I turned to Mom. "Why did you do that?" I said.

"What did I do?"

"You embarrassed me, you embarrassed Joe. You practically twisted his arm and forced him into walking to school with me."

Mom just smiled. "He didn't say no, did he?" she said.

11

THE LUNCH CRUNCH

Joe was standing on my corner, just like he'd promised. We started walking toward school.

"Look," I said to clear the air, "I'm sorry if my mom forced you into meeting me. She gets that way sometimes."

"My mom too," said Joe. "No problem."

"I just wanted you to know it wasn't my idea."

"I have to walk this way to school anyway," Joe said. "So we might as well walk together."

We walked about a block in silence, then Joe spoke up. "Can I ask you a question? Why are you hanging out with Phil Steinkraus?"

I shrugged. "The reason? Because he's the only kid in school who wants to be my friend."

"Do you like the guy?"

"Well," I said, "I don't hate him."

Joe gave me a sideways look. "You know Phil Steinkraus is nuts, don't you?"

"He's pretty tough," I said.

"And he's stupid."

"No," I said, "that's wrong. He's not stupid at all."

"Face it," said Joe, "the guy's a maniac."

"I wouldn't go that far," I said. "He is different, though."

"Different?" said Joe. "Yeah, like a lighted stick of dynamite is different."

"Nobody ever spent two minutes with the guy," I said, "so how do they know? He's not that bad."

Joe didn't reply to that, but I could see him thinking about it. We crossed Oak Street, then Maple. "If you want to make friends in school," said Joe, "you'll have to dump Phil Steinkraus. Kids see you and Steinkraus together and they think, *Hey, this Baker kid must be really weird.* You'll never make friends that way."

"Is that fair?" I asked.

"Maybe, or maybe not. But that's the way things are. Your friend Phil Steinkraus has beaten up half the kids in school."

"Phil Steinkraus has not done me any harm," I said.

"Yet," said Joe, pointing a finger in the air.

Our class was lining up in the yard when we got to school. Then the bells clanged and we started going inside. "Let's talk some more at lunch," said Joe.

Mom was a little more organized this week, so I had a packed lunch in my knapsack. A peanut butter and jelly sandwich, an orange, two cookies, and a frozen apple juice I hoped would thaw in time for lunch. It meant I didn't have to get on the long lunch-line at all.

Joe and I walked downstairs together when the lunch break came. Joe had a metal lunchbox, not a paper bag like me. We found a table and sat down. Libby Klein, Mike Marder, and a few other classmates came over and joined us.

Off in the corner of the lunchroom, at his usual empty table, Phil Steinkraus was looking at me. I gave him a friendly wave.

I was wondering what Joe had in his lunchbox. I kind of hoped it would be Chinese food he might want to share. But it turned out to be tuna fish on white bread.

The other kids were talking about Libby's birthday party. It made me feel sad, just a touch, because I didn't know Libby well enough to be invited. Carrie White was sitting at the far end of the table with a boy named Jimmy Rossillo. She winked at me and I smiled back. Her eyestuff was brown today.

"Tell me about Carrie White," I asked Joe.

"Not much to tell," he said. "She likes boys a lot."

"That much I know."

"She's into makeup and jewelry, wears new earrings every day, and she always has a boyfriend. Since second grade she's had about ten of them."

"Including you?" I asked.

Joe grinned. "No, so far I've been lucky."

"How about the kid sitting with her, Jimmy?"

"A long story," Joe said. "Jimmy's parents got divorced a couple of years ago and he was bad for a while. Always getting into fights and having lots of trouble in school. But lately he's been okay."

"My folks are getting a divorce," I said, "and things have been pretty horrible."

Just then Joe and I both felt a strong hand on our shoulders. "Hi, guys," said Phil Steinkraus. He was standing right behind us and his fingers were digging into our shoulders. "I thought you were supposed to have lunch with me, Marky," said Phil.

I reached up and shoved Phil's hand off my shoulder. "I didn't say I would."

"Is that right?" Phil said.

"Yes, that's right."

Phil's mouth swept back into that wolf grin I'd come to know. "Just like I thought," Phil said, "another one-dollar friend."

I looked into Phil's eyes, but I kept my mouth shut.

"I don't think you're really my friend," Phil said. "Is that right, or what?"

I was afraid to say anything.

"Not a friend at all," Phil said. "In fact, Marky, I don't think I like you anymore."

All the kids at our table had stopped eating and were watching Phil and me. So were most of the kids in the whole lunchroom.

Suddenly Phil leaned down and with the back of his hand swept Joe's lunchbox off the table so it clattered to the floor. "Oops," said Phil with his wolf's grin, "look what happened by accident. I'm so sorry, Joey babe."

Joe sat very still. He made no move to get up and go fetch his lunchbox.

"Ain't you gonna do something about it, Joey babe? Or are you too chicken?" Phil asked. He seemed to be enjoying himself.

Joe didn't move a hair, or even look at Phil.

That's when Libby Klein got to her feet, walked over to

where Joe's lunchbox had fallen, and picked it up. Then she brought it back and put it on the table next to Joe.

"Libby babe," Phil said. "How's it going?"

"Get out of here, birdbrain," Libby said.

Phil stared at Libby for a second, still grinning. "If you weren't a girl . . ." he said.

"Beat it," said Libby.

Phil gave Libby a nod of the head. Then he stuck a finger in front of my nose. "You I'm gonna see when school's over," he said to me. "I'm gonna punch your nose so far through the top of your head you'll never be able to wear a hat, boy. You got a hard lesson to learn, Marky."

Phil stretched himself up even taller than he was and stuck out his chest. Then he turned and sort of swaggered away.

"Don't let him scare you," Libby said to me. "He talks a lot, but if you stand up to him he runs away."

My eyes caught those of the other boys at the table. Joe, Jimmy, Mike Marder, Steve Adolphus, Ned Robbins. Not one word passed between us, but I could see from the way they looked that they didn't agree with Libby. We were all scared of Phil Steinkraus.

"Listen," Joe said quietly to me, "about walking home together. Maybe it's not such a good idea."

12

SHOWDOWN AT THE O.K. CORRAL

School was over after Mr. Pangalos's social studies class. We were working on ancient civilizations. Tonight we all had to read about the Sumerians and answer the quiz at the end of that chapter in our textbook.

I began collecting my things and kids started leaving. As I was stuffing books into my knapsack, Joe came over to me. "Are you okay?" he said.

"Sure, I'm fine."

"Maybe it would be a good idea to hang around inside school for a while," he said.

I kept packing my knapsack.

"Like maybe for an hour?"

"Why don't I stay here for the rest of the day?" I said for a joke. "Maybe I'll sleep here tonight."

Joe didn't think that was funny. His face was so serious. "You know what I mean," he said. "Maybe Phil Steinkraus will get tired of waiting for you and he'll go away."

"Joe," I said, "you can go home if you like."

Joe just stood there.

"Look," I said, "I'm not afraid of that jerk," which was a plain flat-out lie. I was halfway scared to death of him.

"Do you mean that?" asked Joe.

"Yep."

"Thanks," Joe said, but he still didn't leave. I could see he wanted to, but his feet didn't move. "I'm sorry, Mark," he said, "but I'm not really too good at fighting."

"Neither am I."

"I never had a fistfight with anyone," Joe said. "Did you?"

"Once," I said, remembering.

"What happened?"

"I got a split lip and it bled a lot."

"How about the other guy?" asked Joe.

"I hit him in the belt buckle and skinned my knuckles. I don't think I hurt him, though."

"Oh," said Joe. By now we were the only kids left in the classroom. "I wish I knew karate," he said.

"Me too."

We stood there looking at each other, not moving toward the door. I was waiting for Joe to go before I headed out. I could see he was really stuck. He wanted to stay with me and yet he was afraid. "Oh, all right," he said, "I'll walk with you. He can't kill the both of us."

I had to smile because Joe looked so scared.

"On the other hand," I said, "maybe he *can* kill us both. He's sure big enough."

Joe's eyes were very wide open behind his glasses. I was just as frightened as he was, but I was doing a better job of hiding it. "Scoot," I said to Joe, "go on home. I don't need anyone to fight my battles for me."

"You really mean that?" Joe asked, his voice getting higher.

"Yes."

"Whew!" Joe exclaimed. "Thanks." He took a step toward the door, then hesitated. "The guy's an animal," he said. "He's a whole lot meaner and stronger than you."

"Just a lean, mean fighting machine," I said.

"Yeah, that too," said Joe. "Well, good luck." He made a little wave with his hand and then left.

I hung around a couple of minutes to give Joe a head start. Then I walked out of the classroom myself. At the first-floor landing of the stairs, where the big window was, I looked out. Phil Steinkraus was waiting for me out at the curb.

Miss DeBoer was in the downstairs hallway when I passed by. "Still here?" she asked me with a smile.

I nodded at her.

"Have a nice day," she said, and walked off toward Mr. Guma's office.

I felt my heart beating hard as I opened the door and went outside onto the steps. Phil Steinkraus saw me and smiled. I went down the steps and turned away from him, walking toward home. It was so late, the crossing guard had already left. There was not one person on the street.

I heard Phil's footsteps coming up behind me, but I didn't stop walking. Then a big hand was on my knapsack and it spun me around. I really expected that a punch in the mouth would be next. I threw my hands up in my face to ward it off.

But Phil Steinkraus was only grinning at me. "Gotcha! You little scaredy-cat."

"What do you want?"

"Put ya dukes up," he said.

"No."

"Take off your knapsack and fight like a man."

"Uh-uh."

"Why not? Are you chicken?"

"Because I'm not a man," I said, "I'm a kid. And fighting you won't prove anything."

"It'll prove I'm stronger than you," he said. That's when Phil punched me smack on the big muscle in my upper arm. It really hurt and I staggered back a step or two.

"Okay, you big jerk!" I yelled at him. "Are you happy now?"

I was rubbing my arm where Phil had hit me. It was throbbing a lot and hurt like crazy. "Right," I said, "you big bag of muscles. So what?"

"I'm bigger than you, I'm stronger than you, and you're nothing but a rotten wimp!" he yelled in my face.

"And you're a big bully," I said.

Phil's nose was right in front of mine. "Here," he said, "smack me one, I won't even stop you. Just hit me once so I can kill you."

It was tempting. I felt my hand clench into a fist, but I didn't raise my arm. Because I knew what would happen next. There would be tiny pieces of the late Mark Baker scattered all over the sidewalk.

"You-are-not-my-friend!" Phil said, poking a hard finger in my chest with every word.

"You got that right," I said back to him. Then I turned around and started walking away.

69

"Hey, wimp!" Phil called after me. "Come back here!"

I got to the corner and crossed the street, walking and not running. Behind me I heard Phil's running feet catching up. Then he grabbed my knapsack and stopped me. I shook myself free.

"How come you didn't have lunch with me?" he said in a calmer voice.

"Because I didn't want to." I began walking again and this time Phil walked alongside me.

"Wimp," he said, but I didn't answer. "Lousy little chicken-coward-gutless-yellowbelly."

I kept my mouth shut and just walked along. Phil walked along with me, calling me every name he could think of. *Names will never harm me,* I thought, *as long as he keeps away from sticks and stones.*

When Phil ran out of curses, he shut up too. We just kept walking along, looking like the best of friends.

"Listen, you jerkhead," Phil said when we were close to Beverly Road, "tomorrow you're gonna have lunch with me."

"Nope."

"Oh, yes, you are. You're gonna have lunch with me every single day."

"No," I said, "we're finished."

"Another one-dollar friend," Phil said in a sneery way.

"Exactly," I said, "and you want to know why? Because it *costs* too much to be your friend."

"Whaddya mean?"

"It costs me any other friend I might have," I said. "Because that's the way you are. You don't want a friend, you want a *slave*. You want me to be your friend only. And never have any others."

"Who do you wanna be friends with?" he asked. "Joey Chang? That nerdy little nothing?"

"Joe's okay," I said. "He's a good guy."

"He's a wimp, like you."

"He's a friend," I said. "And I'm going to make a lot of other friends too. And if you don't like it, you can go take a flying flop at the moon."

We'd almost reached Beverly Road by now, close to home.

"You really wanna be friends with Joey and Libby and Michael? All those jerks? They're a bunch of wimps. I could beat up any one of them. Or all of them together."

"Probably," I said.

"I hate those kids," Phil said. "Not one of them ever wanted to be my friend. And they all think they're so smart."

"Some of them are," I said.

Now we'd reached the corner. My house was just across the street.

Phil grabbed hold of my arm, right where it was hurting. "Come on into the A & P," he said. He started pulling me along and I couldn't shake his grip.

We went through the doors that open automatically when you step on the rubber pad. Phil half pulled and half shoved me over to the checkout stations, then let go of my arm. There was a skinny blond woman checker packing groceries into a plastic bag. She looked at us and when she smiled there was a small space between her front teeth. "Hey, Philly," she said.

"Hi, Ma," said Phil Steinkraus.

13

ℐN MINNIE'S KITCHEN

"This is my friend, Marky," Phil said.

"Pleased to meet you," said Mrs. Steinkraus.

"Hi," I said.

"I'm always glad to meet one of Philly's friends," she said.

"What's for dinner?" Phil asked her.

"Hamburgers."

"Again?" said Phil in a whiny-baby voice I'd never heard him use before.

"And those crispy fries you like," said Mrs. Steinkraus. "And I'll bring home one of those Boston cream pies too."

"Okay," said Phil. "Will you be late?"

"The usual time," Phil's mom said. "You run on home now and tell Candy I want her to make coffee and a salad, you hear? And I don't want to see any of her beauty stuff on the table when I get home. Tell her to have the table set, understand?"

"Okay," Phil said.

"And you stay away from my beer, Philly, you got that?"

"Yeah."

"I catch you drinking beer again, I'll box your ears for you, hear me?"

"Okay, okay," Phil said in a whiny way.

"See you later, then," said Mrs. Steinkraus. She turned away from us and began checking out the next person in line.

Phil took hold of my arm and drew me away toward the windows. "Let's go to your house," he said.

"No."

"Then walk me home."

"No."

Phil made a face. "I'm sorry I hit you," he said. "I didn't mean nothing by it."

"It still hurts," I said.

Phil considered that for a moment. Then he asked me: "Are you gonna have lunch with me tomorrow or not?"

"Not," I said. "Unless you want to come sit at my table."

"Not with those wimps," he said, "no way." He turned away from me then and walked out through the automatic doors. I watched through the windows as he crossed the street and turned the corner, knowing that something final had happened between us. Phil still wanted to be my friend, but I was finished with him. Joe was right: Phil was like a stick of dynamite that could explode at any moment.

That's when I heard a voice I knew. When I turned around I saw the old woman who lived in my building. She was at the checkout counter, talking with Mrs. Steinkraus. "How are you today, Minnie?" I heard Phil's mom asking.

"The same, Hannah," said the old woman. "That was your boy, Philly, wasn't it? He's getting so big."

"Big and bad, just like his old man, God rest his soul."

The old woman saw me at the window and called out: "Yoo-hoo, sonny!"

I walked over to the checkout and said hello to her.

"This is Marky, Philly's friend," said Mrs. Steinkraus. "And this is Minnie Olson, one of my best customers."

"Mrs. Olson lives in my building," I said.

"No," said Minnie Olson, "you live in *my* building because I was there first. And you're just in time to help me carry my packages."

I waited while Mrs. Steinkraus packed Minnie's items into three bags. I picked up two of them.

"So," said Minnie Olson as we went through the doors, "your name is Marky and your last name is Baker, right?"

"Mark," I said, "not Marky, and how come you know my name?"

We crossed the street as the traffic light turned green.

"I don't miss much," Minnie said with a smile. "Because I'm a nosy old lady and I got nothing to do except listen to gossip and look out my window. And Philly Steinkraus is a friend of yours?"

"Ex-friend," I said. "We just had a fight."

"Goodness, that's exciting!" Minnie exclaimed. "A fight with hitting and punching?"

"One punch," I said.

"And who hit who?"

"Phil was the puncher," I said. "I was the punchee."

"And what was this about, may I ask?"

"It's a long story," I said.

"And here I am with nothing but time on my hands," she said.

We went inside the building and Minnie got out her key to open the inner door. "Come, sweetie," she said to me. "You'll help me inside my apartment with my packages and I'll give you a nice glass of milk and cookies."

Minnie's apartment was exactly like mine directly overhead. Except that Minnie's furniture and things were completely different, of course, so it didn't look anything the same. She had drapes and curtains on the windows that made the place much darker than my apartment. And there were lots of pictures of kids in small picture frames on top of everything, including the refrigerator in the kitchen.

She kept asking me questions about Phil and I answered her. Minnie reminded me so much of my Grandma Rose, who died when I was eight. Grandma Rose always wanted to know what was going on with me and my friends. She was a great listener.

After Minnie put the groceries away, she poured a glass of milk for me. "I can offer you only Oreos today," she said, "because I didn't know I was going to have company. And such a handsome young man, besides. Do you like Oreos?"

"Yes."

"Me too. Do you like to lick off the cream inside them first? That's what I do."

She put a bunch of cookies on a plate and made a cup of tea for herself. Then she sat down at the kitchen table with me. "It's not big news that you had a fight with Philly," she said. "That boy fights with everyone."

75

I told Minnie all about Phil and me, and how he didn't know how to treat a friend.

"No father in the house," she said, "that's why. Philly's father died when he was just a baby. Hannah does her best, but a boy needs a father or he can grow up wild."

"I don't have a father in the house either," I said.

"He died?"

"No, my parents are getting divorced."

Minnie stopped licking the cream off her cookie. "Divorce," she said, "the curse of modern times. I'll bet you cried plenty."

"I did," I said.

"Of course you did, poor thing."

"But not so much anymore."

"And you see your father?"

"Sundays," I said, "but not every Sunday. Sometimes Dad is busy or something."

"That pretty, slim woman I see leaving every morning. That's your mother?"

"Yes. Her name is Joan. She works from nine to five-thirty."

"And you're alone every day after school," Minnie said, shaking her head. "Is this any way to raise a child, I ask you? No wonder we got crime and punishment all over."

"I'm getting used to it," I said.

"Believe me," said Minnie, "it wasn't like this in my time. I was home every day for my girls. But now we got modern times and modern problems and it looks like kids come last."

It was very nice sitting in Minnie's kitchen, talking to her. She was a very sweet woman. I found out she had two married daughters, five grandchildren, and a husband who'd died ten years before. She showed me a whole photo album with pic-

76

tures of her grandkids. "And both my girls went to live in California," she said. "As far away from me as they could get. Do they care how lonely I am? Do they care I get to see my grandchildren only once in a blue moon?"

I finished my milk and looked at my watch.

"Here I am, bending your ear, and you probably got a million things to do," said Minnie. "Next time you come, believe me, I'll have cookies home-baked for you, not from a box."

"They were great," I said, picking up my knapsack.

"And you are sweet as sugar," said Minnie. Before I knew what happened, she grabbed me and kissed my cheek. "Don't you be a stranger, now," she said as she let me out the door. "You come visit me anytime you're lonely, you hear?"

"I will," I promised.

When I got upstairs I could hear the telephone ringing inside my apartment. I opened the front door fast and ran to the kitchen phone. I thought it must be Mom, checking if I was home. But when I picked up the phone, it was Joe.

"Mark? Is that you?"

"Yep."

"Whew!" said Joe. "I was afraid Phil Steinkraus killed you."

14

DUMPLINGS

Phil Steinkraus was not in school the next day. Which was a good thing, as far as I was concerned.

Joe and me walked home together. We got to the corner where we had to part company, but I didn't feel like being alone. "Come on up to my place," I said.

"Can't do it."

"Why not?"

"Because I have to work later," Joe said.

"You have a *job*?" I couldn't believe it.

"From about five to nine o'clock every day," Joe said. "Delivering take-out orders. If you and your mom order food from us, I'll be the guy ringing your doorbell."

"That's great," I said.

"I don't know if it's great," Joe said. "The bad thing is, I have to get my homework done as soon as I get home. And I have to eat dinner really early."

"Is it fun?"

"No," said Joe, "it's work. Especially in the rain. Or when it gets cold in the winter. Or when some idiot orders a bunch of food and sends it to a stranger for a joke."

"You're kidding," I said. "Nobody could be so mean."

Joe smiled. "You'd be surprised. There are some real weirdos out there. On the other hand, I have my regulars. People who order every week, sometimes twice a week. Some of them give me a really big tip when I deliver. In fact, one of my regulars lives in your building. Mrs. Olson on the ground floor."

"I know her," I said. "She's very nice."

"She sure is," said Joe. "She never tips me less than a dollar. And once she gave me five bucks."

"Wow."

"She said it was her birthday."

"Wait a minute," I said. "It was *her* birthday and she gave *you* a five-dollar tip?"

"I think she was lonely," Joe said. "She asked me to stick around, so I sat with her while she had her soup. That Minnie sure can talk. Then when I said I had to go, she stuck five dollars in my hand."

Joe was about to walk away from me toward home when I asked if I could go with him. "We could do our homework together," I said.

"I don't know," Joe said with a shrug. "My family is a little funny, Mark."

"Not any funnier than mine," I said. "They don't live together anymore and they can't even stand the sight of each other."

"Okay," Joe decided. "But look—you have to remember

that sometimes they make mistakes in English. Especially my uncle Han."

"What difference does that make?"

"I'm just saying."

"They're your family, aren't they?"

Joe nodded and we began to walk. "Sometimes I get a little embarrassed when they say something wrong," he said. "Especially to kids I know."

Just outside the Jade Garden was a bicycle that had a deep metal basket attached to the front handlebars. "The old delivery vehicle," Joe said. "If I got paid by the mile I'd be a millionaire."

"How much do you get paid, anyway?"

Joe laughed. "Zip-o," he said. "But I keep the tips."

"You mean you work for nothing? That's unfair."

"It's a family business," Joe said. "My parents work very hard, seven days a week. I have to do my part, don't I?"

We went inside the restaurant, which had no customers at this hour. I followed Joe toward the back. There was a big round table there, sort of hidden behind a low partition. Mishi was sitting there, working on a coloring book.

"Hi, Mishi," Joe said, but she didn't even look up.

We walked behind Mishi to look at her work. She was coloring a picture of Little Bo Peep and each of her sheep was a different color.

"I never saw a purple sheep," Joe said. "Or a red one."

"Aren't they pretty?" Mishi said.

"Just like you," said Joe.

"No," she said, "I'm prettier."

"Mom, I'm home!" Joe called out.

Joe's mom poked her head through the swinging door that led to the kitchen.

"I brought Mark home with me," Joe said. "We're going to do our homework together."

Mrs. Chang smiled at me. "First, milk and cookie," she said, and she disappeared behind the door.

Joe and I unloaded our knapsacks and sat down at the table. In about a minute Mrs. Chang came along with a tray that had two glasses of milk on it and a plate of cookies. I really expected to see almond or fortune cookies, but there were only chocolate-covered grahams.

When we finished our snacks I remembered something. I used the pay telephone on the wall and called Mom at her office. I told her where I was and that I'd be home later.

We did our math homework together and then started on social studies. While we were working, Mrs. Chang and Uncle Han came out of the kitchen and sat down with us at the big table. They had a tray of what looked like flattened round disks of dough. About a minute later Joe's dad came out of the kitchen and handed them a big bowl of chopped meat.

Joe introduced me to his dad, who wiped his hands on his white apron before shaking hands with me. "Friend of Joe," he said, "very good."

Han and Mrs. Chang started scooping up spoonfuls of the chopped meat, put each spoonful on a disk of dough, then rolled and pinched the dough into a little bundle. When they had finished rolling and pinching and shaping, each bundle became a little stuffed crescent moon that looked really neat. I asked Mrs. Chang what they were called.

"Jao tze," she said, "dumplings."

81

"Some people call them Peking ravioli," said Joe.

"I think I had them once, a long time ago," I said.

"They get steamed or fried," said Joe, "and they're pretty tasty. Except when Mom serves them for breakfast."

Mrs. Chang smiled at Joe. "Better than cornflakes, you silly child."

"Wrong," said Joe. He turned to me. "We have this running disagreement. Mom hates it when I like something American better than Chinese. I keep telling her I was born here, not in Canton."

Meanwhile, Han and Mrs. Chang kept working as Joe and I did our homework. I kept looking at how quickly each dumpling got finished. The big tray was already half filled with those little crescent moons. And each one was so neat and perfect, you would think they were made by a machine, not people.

"How do you do that?" I asked Mrs. Chang.

"Doing it since I'm a little girl," she said.

"Could I try making one?" I asked.

"You?" she said with a smile.

"I could try. It looks like fun."

"Okay," she said, "but first you must wash hands."

I went off to the gents' room and did that, then came back to the table and sat down next to Mrs. Chang. She took a disk of dough about three inches across and placed it in the palm of my hand. Then she put a spoonful of the filling in the center of it.

I started folding one edge over the other and pinching it, but it was hard to do. Mrs. Chang showed me how to hold it against the thumb and forefinger of one hand and kind of push and pinch with the same fingers of the other hand. I kept doing it, but the filling began to squish out.

I pushed the filling back in and kept on pinching the dough closed until I finished it. Sort of. It looked ugly and wrinkled and was kind of a ball.

Mrs. Chang thought it was funny.

"I made a full moon," I said, "not a crescent."

She took the dumpling and fixed it up in about five seconds. "See," she said, "not bad. You keep doing it you get good like me."

"Yeah," I said. "If I did it every day for about a year."

Mrs. Chang giggled, then patted my cheek. "Nice boy," she said. "It's good for Joe to make a friend."

I smiled back at her, and this is what I thought: Mrs. Chang sounded exactly like my mom.

15

A DAY WITH DAD

I hung out with Joe after school a couple more days that week. I didn't make any more dumplings, though. Joe was a chess player, a game I knew nothing about. So Joe began to teach me the moves and he loaned me a beginner's book to study at home.

That Saturday, Mom and I went shopping and came home to work on my room. It had been kind of a mess since we'd moved in, with cartons of my stuff piled into an empty corner. We hung curtains on the window and put down a big cotton shag rug that covered most of the floor. Then we rearranged the furniture and put the new lamp we'd bought on my night table so I could read in bed if I wanted to.

The best part was that we could make more room for me by finally getting rid of all those cartons. I put the posters I'd always had in my room: Charlie Chaplin, Kirby Puckett, and a big one of Savage Towels, a group whose music I liked.

That night we had dinner at the Jade Garden. Joe kept

coming in and going back with orders to deliver. When we were almost finished eating, Mrs. Chang came over and talked to us. She told Mom what a nice boy I was, which was a bit embarrassing. And then a few minutes later Uncle Han brought me a big plate of ice cream for dessert, which was free.

On the way out Mom stood and talked with Mrs. Chang while Mom was paying our bill. They talked and talked so long, I went outside on the street to wait. Joe came riding up on his delivery vehicle. "Great night for tips," he said. "It must be the full moon."

Mom finally came outside and we walked the two blocks home. "Mrs. Chang really likes you," she said.

"I like her too. She's nice."

"And she said that she's very glad that Joe has a new friend at last."

That didn't sound right to me. "What did she mean, 'at last'?"

"I don't know," said Mom, "but that's what she said."

I thought about that when I was in bed with the lights out. Joe had been going to our school since kindergarten. He knew all the kids inside out. So why didn't he have friends?

Maybe, I thought, because he worked so much after school, so he didn't go to anyone else's house. Was I the only one Joe had ever invited home with him after school? Did he care that much about how his parents spoke English?

Then I started worrying about whether Dad was going to show up the next morning. Or would he call at the last minute and say he couldn't make it? He'd done that before.

Dad was only a half hour late that Sunday. It was a sunny day and warm for September. He came into the apartment with a big smile on his face and gave me a hug. "You are looking really great, kiddo," he said.

"Hello, Bill," Mom said. She was already dressed, even though it wasn't even ten o'clock.

"How are you doing?" Dad asked her.

"Just peachy," Mom said in a funny way.

Dad nodded. "I'm keeping Mark through dinner."

"Lovely," said Mom.

"It's such a great day, I thought we'd spend part of it out-doors."

I gave Mom a kiss good-bye, and she said I should take a sweater with me. I went back to my room and got my sweat-shirt jacket out of my closet. When I came back to the kitchen, I could see how angry Mom was. She was saying something about a crow, or maybe it was escrow, and telling Dad he'd better live up to his agreement or else.

Dad kept telling Mom to take it easy, that she'd get every penny that was coming to her, but not until things were set-tled.

When they finally noticed I was standing there, they shut up. I was so upset and angry at them, I walked right out the door without saying good-bye to Mom. I flew downstairs in a rush and waited outside by Dad's pickup.

We had breakfast at the Hojo again. Dad was very quiet on the way there and while we ate. He didn't finish his pancakes, either, but drank a lot of coffee and smoked cigarettes.

I think that's when I began to stop thinking about Dad and Mom getting back together again. I'd have to be pretty stupid to keep thinking that was going to happen, when they couldn't stand being in the same room together for two minutes.

86

The three of us would never be one family again. Never. That was the way it was going to be. Forever.

"Look," Dad said when we were back in the pickup and rolling down the highway, "I want you to forget what you saw between your mom and me. We shouldn't fight in front of you. I'm sorry."

"Right."

"Your mom and me," he said, "we don't really hate each other, Mark. Not the way it looks now, anyway."

"Well," I said, "it's pretty clear you don't love each other."

Dad made a noise halfway between a grunt and a laugh. "True."

"And one of these days you'll be divorced, right?"

"In a few months," said Dad. "By the end of the year, I guess."

"Yeah, right," I said, "that's what I thought."

"But that doesn't mean we're going to stop thinking about you, Mark, or stop loving you. Even though we live apart."

"I know," I said as the pickup went over a highway overpass.

"Maybe sometime later on you'll want to live with me," Dad said. "Right now it wouldn't be good. You need your mom more than me at your age."

"I need you too," I said.

"I know that."

"I miss you a lot," I said.

I wanted to say more, but I didn't. I just looked out the window. I'd called Dad three times this week and got his phone machine all three times. Dad had called me back only once, on Friday night to say he'd see me today.

THE SQUEAKY WHEEL

How come he didn't call me more? Why wasn't he home when I called? I really wanted to ask him about it, but I didn't want to sound like I was nagging him.

We had a good morning and afternoon that day. We walked along Riverfront Park and later went to the museum there. They had an exhibit on the Indians of the plains. It was neat. There was a real tepee you could go into, and lots of hatchets and war clubs.

Later on we sat under a tree and had hot dogs and sodas Dad bought from a vendor. Then we went to Dad's place.

He called it a garden apartment, although there wasn't a garden anyplace near it. There was just a small lawn out front and a big parking lot in the rear. Dad's apartment was up two flights of stairs and it was tiny. You could hardly turn around in the kitchen. And there was only one small bedroom and a little living room that faced the parking lot.

"How about we have a catch?" Dad asked me.

"Great!" I said. "But with what? My glove and ball are back in my room."

"Well," said Dad, "I've been thinking about that. Let's take a look in this closet here."

I opened the front hall closet. Up on the shelf was a brand-new baseball glove and a new ball!

"Dad, it's great," I said as I put the glove on my hand and pounded the ball into it. "Thanks a lot." I gave Dad a hug and he reached down and ruffled my hair.

"It seemed silly to make you wait until Christmas," Dad said. "Now let me find my old mitt and we'll be in business."

We went out front and started tossing the ball back and forth. I don't know why, but I felt terrific. We threw for a while, then Dad gave me some high tosses—pop-ups—to handle. It was just like we did it back home, when we'd go out in the driveway or the backyard to throw the baseball around.

We played ball for about an hour, then went back upstairs and watched the end of the football game on TV.

"Now, Mark," Dad said when the game was over, "I've made plans for dinner and I'd like you to agree, okay?"

"Sure."

"We'll have your favorite, Italian food."

"At Nino's?" I asked. That was the place we always went when we lived here. I loved their spaghetti with meat sauce.

Dad smiled. "You guessed it."

"Terrific," I said, "let's go."

"We will," Dad said. "But first we'll pick up my friend, Trudy, and her little girl. I'd like you to meet them. And then we'll go to Nino's together."

I saw the way Dad was looking at me and I said, "Okay," even though I really didn't want to. I saw Dad only once a week. I didn't want to share him with other people. But we'd had such a good day up to now, I didn't want to spoil it.

"You'll like Trudy," Dad said, "and little Tiffany too. They're really eager to meet you, Mark, because I've told them so much about you. I'm sure you'll like them."

I wasn't sure I'd like them at all. Maybe because I hated them already. But it seemed like I didn't have any choice.

16

PSGHETTI

When we pulled up outside Trudy's house, Dad looked me over and sort of combed down my hair with his fingers. Then we went up on the porch and rang the bell. A little girl in overalls and a T-shirt opened the door and stared out at us. She had dark hair that ended in a ponytail, with a white ribbon to tie it up.

"Hi, Tiff," Dad said. He reached down and picked her up and she gave him a kiss on his cheek. "Say hi to Mark," Dad told her. The little girl put her face into Dad's shoulder and wouldn't look at me. "She's shy," Dad said.

Trudy came walking to the door. She had dark hair, like Tiffany's, and dark brown eyes. "Well," she said with a smile, "you must be the famous Mark."

"Hi," I said.

"You're taller than I thought," she said. "And even more handsome than your dad said you were."

I didn't know what to say, so I said nothing.

We went inside the house. It was a nice place, with carpet all over and the walls painted white. Everything looked new and clean. Dad put Tiffany down on the floor and she scooted over to her mom and held on to her skirt. Trudy got a sweater for Tiffany and a jacket for herself and we left the house.

We couldn't all fit in Dad's pickup, so we went to the restaurant in Trudy's Plymouth. Dad sat up front with Trudy, I sat in the back with Tiffany. She kept peeking over at me, then looking away. Every time she peeked at me I gave her a little wave with my hand and said hi. After a while she began to have a smile on her face each time I said it, so I kept it up.

We got seated at a table in the back of Nino's and Tiffany was put into a baby seat. I felt really funny being there with people I didn't know; Nino's was one of the places where I always went with Mom and Dad. We've had dinner there so many Friday nights, I couldn't begin to count them all. We were always one happy family at Nino's.

I ordered the spaghetti I liked and Tiffany said she wanted spaghetti too. But she called it "psghetti." She ate it funny, sucking one strand at a time into her tiny mouth and making a little noise. She ate only a little bit, then she quit and watched me eat. After a while she said my name: "Mock."

"Mark," I said.

"Mock." She nodded, sure she had my name right.

"You've made a hit," Trudy said to me. "Tiff is usually too shy to speak to someone new."

"Especially on the first date," Dad said, which made Trudy laugh.

We went back to Trudy's house after dinner, then Dad and I got back into the pickup. I had a lot of thoughts in my head as

---

91

we drove through the dark toward home. I didn't say much, though. But when Dad pulled up in front of the apartment house to let me off, I blurted out the one thing I couldn't stop thinking about. "You're going to marry Trudy, aren't you?"

Dad's mouth opened in surprise. "Hey, that's a big jump," he said.

"Are you?" I asked.

"I can't marry anyone," Dad said. "I'm still married to your mom."

"But how about next year? When you won't be?"

Dad sighed. "Who can tell?" he said. "I'm just getting to know Trudy right now. It's too soon to say what's going to happen."

"But it's possible," I said.

"Anything's possible," Dad said. "The world could end tomorrow."

"Come on, Dad."

"Don't go getting yourself upset about something that may never happen," he said. "I mean that, Mark."

"Okay," I said. "But I want to know what's coming."

"Don't we all," Dad said.

"I've had enough surprises lately," I said.

"Well," said Dad, "you're my son and I'm your dad and that's not going to change. No matter what."

He gave me a kiss on the cheek then and we said good-night. I reminded him to call me during the week and he said he'd try. He waited in the pickup until I went through the inside door of the house.

Mom was in the living room when I let myself into our apartment. She was sitting on the couch with her eyeglasses on and the Sunday newspapers next to her. "Hello, there," she said. "Did you have a nice day?"

I sat down on the couch beside her and put my new baseball glove on the floor. "Look," I said, "I gotta know something right now. Are you going to start going out on dates with strange men?"

Mom's eyes widened. "Whoa, there," she said, "you're way ahead of me."

"But are you?"

"What is this, the third degree?"

"I'm asking you a question, Mom. Are you going to start dating men and will you get married again?"

"Ah-hah!" she cried out, raising one finger in the air.

"So what's the answer?" I said.

"First of all, calm down." She shoved her glasses on top of her head. "You seem upset about this and I don't know why. Did something happen today with Dad? Did he say something about getting married again?"

"I don't want to talk about that," I said. "Why can't you just answer me, yes or no?"

"Because it's not that simple, sweetie. And I can't talk about it without a cup of tea."

She got up from the couch and I followed her into the kitchen while she started making tea. I poured half a glass of milk for myself and sat down at the table. I knew my mom. She would not answer the question until she was good and ready. Sometimes it made me angry, like now, but there wasn't a thing I could do to make her talk.

When her tea was ready she put in a touch of milk and a spoonful of sugar and brought it to the table. She sat down and stared into her mug of tea for a while. Then she looked at me again and grinned. "What was that question again?" she said.

I knew she was teasing, so I just stared at her.

"Okay," she went on, still grinning, "will I go out on dates with strange men? Answer: If they're strange I won't go anywhere near them."

"That's not funny," I said.

"Perhaps not," she said. "But truthfully, dating is not on my agenda right now."

"But what if you meet some nice guy?" I asked.

"Who knows?" She took a sip of her tea. "Look, Mark, I have a lot on my mind right now. You, the new job, the apartment, the settlement with your dad, selling the old house. I'm just taking one thing at a time."

"What about getting married again?" I asked. "Will I have a stepfather?"

"Honey," Mom said, "I am not a fortune-teller and I don't have a crystal ball. I used to think I'd be married to your dad forever, so you see what I know." She sipped her tea again and looked out the dark kitchen window. "But I'll have to say this . . . *if* some nice guy came along . . . and *if* he wanted to get married . . . and *if* I really felt something for him . . . then, *yes,* I'd probably get married again."

"I knew it," I said.

"But that doesn't mean I'm getting married tomorrow," she said. "Or even that I'll start dating again. So stop worrying."

"But I am worried," I said.

We looked into each other's eyes for a moment.

"Honey," she said, "I'm not going to do anything to make you unhappy."

When she said that, I felt a little shiver pass through me. I didn't think Mom was lying. Not exactly. But she and Dad had already made me very unhappy. So why should I believe her now?

We talked a little while longer and then I went to bed.

I lay in my bed in the dark, the new curtains swaying as a cool breeze came through the window. My mind kept racing along and I couldn't do a thing to slow it down.

Dad would marry Trudy, I thought. Tiffany would be my stepsister and Trudy my stepmother.

Mom would meet someone and get married again. And Mr. I-don't-know-who would be my stepdad.

Too many changes were going to happen and I found it all scary. Where would I fit in? Would I end up living in Trudy's neat house? Would I go on living with Mom and her new husband? And where would that be?

Before I got more scared, I must have fallen asleep.

17

CARRIE AND JIMMY

Mr. Pangalos told us we would have to do a long report on the Sumerians. Down front, Joe turned in his seat and nodded at me. I winked back at him, meaning we'd work together on the report.

But it didn't turn out that way. Mr. Pangalos said he would *assign* committees of three, which made everyone groan aloud, because they wanted to work with their friends. I got Carrie White and Jimmy Rossillo as my report partners.

We all shifted seats when Mr. Pangalos gave us ten minutes to get organized. "Who's good at writing?" Jimmy asked. "Because I stink."

"I'll do it," I said.

"Great," said Jimmy. "I'm going to do all the artwork. It's the only thing I like to do."

I wasn't going to argue with Jimmy. I am a person who is totally terrible in art. I could draw a horse and it would look like a car. And vice versa.

"I have a good encyclopedia at home," Carrie said. "We can use it for our report."

"Okay," Jimmy said, "then we'll work at your house."

"Why should it be my house?" Carrie said. "I could bring the encyclopedia to your house just as easily."

"Fine," said Jimmy, who didn't seem to be interested in anything except drawing pictures. "We'll meet at my house."

"We could work at my house," I volunteered. "It's not a house, though, it's an apartment."

Jimmy shrugged, as if to say he didn't care one way or the other. Carrie kept looking down at my fingers, then she reached out and grabbed my left hand. "Your nails are fabulous!" she said. "Do you do them yourself?"

"No," I said, pulling my hand away.

"Then who does them? Your mom?"

"Of course not," I said.

Carrie wouldn't give up. She grabbed my hand again and looked at it closely. "Somebody does your nails," she said. "Who?"

"The same person who does Michael Jackson's nails," I said.

Carrie gave me a funny look, but Jimmy burst out laughing. We talked about our report until the period ended. It was very clear to me that I'd do all the work on our report, Jimmy would do all the artwork and illustrations, and Carrie would only get in the way.

At lunch I sat down with Joe, as usual, but Carrie came along and slid into a seat on the other side of me. "Come on, now," she said, "tell the truth. Who really does your nails?"

I told her the whole story of my afternoon with Phil Steinkraus and his sister. Including how she wanted to put makeup and lipstick on my face.

"I can see why," Carrie said. "You're really cute, Mark."

Compliments like that get me embarrassed. I never know what to say. "I'm not cute," I said.

"You are, really," Carrie insisted. "You're probably the best-looking boy in our class."

Words failed me, so I just crossed my eyes, stuck out my tongue, and made the gooniest face I could.

"I want you to go to Libby's party with me," said Carrie.

"We've been through this already."

"I know that," said Carrie.

"I really don't want a girlfriend."

"I know that too," she said. Carrie looked at my fingers again. "I wish I had nails like yours," she said, making me think even more that she was a complete airhead. Her eyestuff was purple-pink today.

Before school ended, the three of us agreed to begin work on our report at my house tomorrow. I'd speak to Mom about it. There was no good reason I couldn't have kids I knew come up to our apartment after school. I wasn't a baby anymore who had to lock himself in behind a door until his mother got home.

I walked home with Joe and we did our homework fast, because I wanted to play chess. Right now I knew how the pieces moved and not much else. We played a couple of games and Joe won very quickly. Then Joe asked Uncle Han to play. Han said he had work to do, so they played what Joe called "blitz" chess. As soon as one player moved, the other player had to make a move without hesitation.

It was amazing to watch.

Han's and Joe's hands flew across the board, moving pieces, taking pieces off, saying "Check." It went so fast, I couldn't figure out why they were doing what they were doing until the endgame.

Han had five pieces left and Joe only two. So Joe quit by laying down his king. "Why can't I ever beat you?" Joe said.

"Maybe someday," said Han.

"When?" asked Joe.

"When Mishi get married," Han said, and he began laughing.

That night we ate home for once and I asked Mom about Carrie and Jimmy coming over to work on our report. I expected an argument but didn't get one. All Mom was worried about was if we had milk and cookies for them.

The next day Jimmy walked home with Joe and me. Carrie was going home to get her encyclopedia, then she'd come over.

I unlocked the door downstairs and Jimmy followed me up to the second floor and into our apartment. He looked around. "Kind of dark and spooky in here," he said before I turned the lights on. "And small," he added. "How many in your family?"

"Just me and my mom." I told Jimmy about my parents getting a divorce soon.

We put our knapsacks down and I got us milk and cookies. "How often do you see your dad?" Jimmy asked.

"On Sundays," I said. "If he remembers or isn't too busy."

"At least you see him. I haven't seen my dad since Christmas. I was supposed to spend the summer with him in San Diego, but he never sent the airplane ticket."

"Does he call you on the phone?" I asked Jimmy.

He shrugged. "Not very often."

"Do you miss him?"

"Yeah," said Jimmy. "But I try not to think about him too much." He chewed on his cookie for a moment. "I don't think he misses me at all."

"Maybe he does."

"He sure doesn't act like it," Jimmy said. "This summer he went to Mexico on a vacation. And he sent me a postcard from down there. When I got it I wanted to start punching walls, I was so mad. I said to myself . . . if Dad had enough money for a vacation, why didn't he pay for my airplane ticket instead?"

I took another cookie.

"Divorce sucks," Jimmy said.

"I'm finding that out."

"Yeah," Jimmy said, "but your dad's still around. At least you get to see him."

"One rotten day a week, that's all."

"That's a lot more than I get," he said.

"And last Sunday Dad dragged me out to dinner with his girlfriend and her baby. I hated it."

"Did you tell him?" asked Jimmy.

"No."

"Why not?"

It was my turn to shrug.

"Mark, don't be a quiet little dope. You've got to speak up. Ask for what you want and carry on until you get it."

"I'm not like that, Jimmy."

"Then learn. First rule of divorce: Parents think of themselves first and you come second. You've got to fight back."

"My folks aren't like that," I said.

Jimmy laughed out loud. "Yeah, right, they're terrific people."

"They are."

Jimmy shook his head. "Everything's fine until they split, Mark. Then nothing's good anymore, believe me. My dad's supposed to send support payments every month, only he's about six months behind right now. The few times he calls me my mom grabs the phone right out of my hand and starts screaming at him."

I swallowed hard, thinking about my own parents, who couldn't be together without fighting. Would they be like Jimmy's folks a year from now?

"Mom's got a saying," said Jimmy. " 'The squeaky wheel gets the grease.' You want something? Learn how to ask for it. Or else forget about it."

"I don't think I can do that," I said.

"Then you better start," Jimmy said. He wiped his mouth with the back of his hand. "You said you hated going out with your dad's girlfriend, right? Tell him about it, Mark. Say you're not gonna do it. Don't be a wimp."

"I'll have to think about that," I said.

That's when the telephone rang. When I picked it up, it was Carrie. "My mom won't let me come over to your house," she said. "So why don't you both come here, okay?"

I told Jimmy what Carrie'd said, and he just smiled. "You know what's between Carrie's ears? Peanut butter and jelly."

I called Mom to let her know where I was going to be, and

then we went to Carrie's house. I took a lot of notes from her encyclopedia and Jimmy copied some drawings. We both knew what Carrie was going to contribute to our report: zilch.

When I finished my homework that night, I kept thinking about what Jimmy had said. Was I really being a wimp?

I never fought with my parents. Mostly because I never had to. Usually I got what I wanted because they wanted to give it to me. Sure, once in a while there was a toy or game or something I wanted that I didn't get. But that was kid stuff.

What did I really want now?

I remember a poem I'd read in a kids' magazine in school.

I asked my folks for a trip to France.
They gave me instead a pair of pants.
And when I asked them for a horse,
I got instead my folks' divorce.

When I read that I thought it was funny. Now I didn't see the humor in it.

What did I really want? I made a list in my mind.

1) No more fighting between them when I was around. It got me completely crazed.
2) More time with Dad. More phone calls. Sometimes I was afraid he'd just disappear.
3) No more Trudy and Tiffany. Dad had six days to see them, he didn't have to do it on Sunday.
4) I had to get my bicycle back. I can't say why my bike was so important to me. I just wanted it.

Maybe Jimmy was right. Maybe I had to start acting like a squeaky wheel to get what I wanted . . . start screaming and yelling and kicking up a fuss.

The trouble was, I'd never acted like that before, and I wasn't sure I knew how.

18

S ECRET STORAGE

I was coming home from school with Joe when we bumped into Minnie Olson on my corner. "Hello, my two handsome boys," she said to us with a smile. "I just happen to have some freshly made brownies still warm from the oven. Who wants to keep an old lady company?"

"I can't," said Joe.

"Come on," I said to Joe, "take a few minutes off for once."

"I have to get home," Joe said, and he walked off toward the Jade Garden.

I followed Minnie into her apartment. In the kitchen she dished out some brownies. When I took my first bite, I couldn't believe how good they were. They had warm and melty chocolate chips in them!

"My secret recipe," Minnie said, watching my smile. "Terrific, huh?"

"Fantastic. Joe doesn't know what he's missing."

"He never gets a minute off," I said. "Isn't there a law against that?"

"Never mind law," said Minnie.

"I wish Joe had time after school to play some basketball with me," I said. "But he's always working, and that isn't right."

"Listen, Mark," said Minnie, "in a family you do what you have to do. We were four sisters in my family. And when our father died, two of us went to work so we could keep our heads above water. That's why I never went past seventh grade in school."

"That's not right either," I said.

"Maybe it's not right," said Minnie, "but it's life. My sister Sarah became a secretary and I worked in a dress shop. And we all survived."

"But maybe if you kept on in school, you could have been something else," I said.

"Like what?"

"I don't know," I said, "—a teacher, maybe, or a scientist."

Minnie started laughing. "Me? A scientist? Mark, that's really funny. I'm happy I can read and write, never mind making a rocket to the moon."

"Maybe you could have," I said. "You're smart as anything."

That got me a big smoochy kiss on my forehead. "Bless your sweetheart," said Minnie. She finished making her tea and sat down at the table with me. "Never mind me," she said. "How are you doing?"

105

"Better," I said.

"I don't see you with Philly anymore. Is that over?"

I nodded.

"I figured," said Minnie. "That boy's got problems." She broke a brownie in half and took a small bite. "You and Joey seem to have hit it off."

"Joe's great," I said, "and he's teaching me chess. But . . . I don't know, I wish I had some other friends. And I wish Joe had time to do other things after school. Like going bike riding. I miss riding my bike."

"So why don't you ride it alone?" asked Minnie.

"Because," I said, "my bike is in my friend Brett's garage, back where I used to live. Mom won't let me keep it in our apartment."

"I don't understand," said Minnie. "Why don't you keep your bike in the storage room?"

Ding-ding! went a little bell in my head. "Storage room? What's that?" I asked.

"My dear boy," said Minnie. She got to her feet. "Come, I'll show you where to keep your bike."

I followed Minnie out of her apartment and onto the street. We walked around the building to the side street, and then to the rear, where there was a low fence with a gate. Minnie opened the gate and we walked through it and down a ramp. You couldn't see it from the side of the building, but there was a basement that had a rear entrance.

"The hall key opens the basement door," Minnie said as she opened it. She turned on the lights and I followed her inside. "You see?" said Minnie. "Every apartment has one of these storage cubicles for keeping baby carriages, bicycles, and whatever."

"And we have one too?"

"Right over here," said Minnie, walking a few steps and pointing to a space fenced in with metal mesh. The door to it had our apartment number on it. "You got room for a lot of things in there," said Minnie, "including your bike. What you need is a good lock for the door."

"Wow!" I said, getting excited. "It's great. Mom doesn't know about this. I can keep my bike down here and just walk it up the ramp to the street."

"Of course," said Minnie. "Just remember to turn off the lights when you leave. And to always keep your cubicle locked, because you never know these days."

I couldn't wait to tell Mom about it. I said good-bye to Minnie, retrieved my knapsack, and ran upstairs to telephone Mom. I thought she'd be so happy for me.

But when I finally got her on the phone, she didn't really sound interested. "Good" was all she said. "Mark, I can't talk now," she went on. "My boss is on my neck and things are crazy around here. I'll see you later."

I was so happy, I could hardly concentrate on my homework. After I'd finished it I paced around the apartment. While I was looking out the front window I saw a big kid coming out of the A & P. It was Phil Steinkraus.

I pulled my head back behind the curtains but kept looking. Phil stopped at the curb and looked up at the front of my building. I had the feeling he was looking for me. Then Phil turned away and began walking down the street. I watched him until he was out of sight.

A little while later I called Dad's number, even though I knew he was probably working and I'd get his message machine.

I waited through the beep and then began talking. "So you see," I concluded, "I can really have my bike here now. Maybe you can go over to Brett's house after work and bring it here tonight. Or tomorrow. Or else we can get it on Sunday. Isn't it great!"

I could hardly wait for Mom to come home.

19

A STORMY NIGHT

Mom came into the apartment boiling mad and almost an hour late. She threw the mail down on the hall table. "This has been one of the worst days of my life," she announced, then she went to the cabinet near the sink and made herself a drink. "I hate my boss, I hate my job, and I hate that horrible computer."

"Hello," I said.

"Hello to you too," she replied. "I haven't got the least idea what's for dinner, so don't ask me." She went off to her room to change her clothes, taking her drink.

I sat at the kitchen table, waiting for her to come back. When she reappeared, she was wearing jeans and a sweatshirt. She'd also finished about half her drink. "Sometimes I'd like to grab hold of that Mr. Harrington and send him to the moon, dead."

"About my bike—"

"Not now!" she barked at me.

I shut right up, which was probably smart. When Mom was in a bad mood she snapped like a turtle. So we just sat in silence for a long while. Then I said, "I really don't care much about dinner either."

"Good."

"Really, I could have anything," I said.

"There's some leftover spaghetti and meatballs," she said. "I could heat it up for you."

"Fine. You don't have to fuss for me tonight."

All of a sudden Mom was crying. She took the bottom of her sweatshirt and dabbed at her eyes. I got up, went around the table, and hugged her. "Hey," I said, "it can't be that bad."

Maybe that was the wrong thing to say, because Mom began sobbing. She grabbed hold of my hands and kissed them, then pulled my head down and cuddled it under her chin. "What would I do without you?" she said in a teary voice.

We stayed like that for a few minutes, Mom hugging me and petting my hair, until she calmed down. Then she kissed my forehead, let me go, and walked over to the sink. She washed her face with cold water and dried it with a paper towel. "Teary time," she said. "I cried in the office too. In the ladies' room."

"What happened?" I asked.

"Disaster. I made a large and stupid mistake I didn't see until it was too late. My boss got nasty about it and I had to stay late and do everything over. I felt like a fool."

"Anybody can make a mistake," I said.

"Not in my office they can't," she said.

In the end Mom warmed the spaghetti and meatballs for me

for dinner. It was okay, except for the inside of the meatballs, which were cold. I didn't mention it. She made herself coffee and ate a few crackers with it. By the end of dinner she seemed to be feeling better.

"Minnie Olson showed me something today," I said. And I told Mom about the storage room in the basement. "It's perfect for my bike, Mom."

"I'll have to see it," she said.

"Let's go downstairs and I'll show it to you." I started to get up.

"Not now," she said, "not tonight. I just want to sit here and finish my coffee."

"Okay," I said. "But take my word for it, it's great. Now I can get my bike out of Brett's garage. I can ride it again."

"Mark," Mom said, "don't get too excited, all right? I don't know if I want you riding your bike around here."

"Why not?" I said. I could feel a burn of anger in my throat.

"I just don't, okay?" she said.

"No," I said, my voice rising. "It's not okay. I want my bike."

"I don't know," Mom said.

"I do!" I insisted. "Why can't I have my bike?"

"Have you looked outside?" she said. "All that traffic on Beverly Road. Including buses."

"I won't be riding my bike on Beverly Road," I said. "I'll ride in the neighborhood. Which is just like where we used to live. You never objected to me riding my bike there."

"But there's a big difference," she said. "I wasn't working then, Mark. I was home."

"So what?"

111

"If you'd had an accident, I could have been there."

"That doesn't make any sense," I said. "I could have had an accident around the corner and you'd never even know about it."

"But I could have been there," she said.

That sounded so dumb to me. I was really getting steamed. "Look," I said, "I will *not* have an accident. You know I'm very careful. I'll *walk* my bike on Beverly Road. Come on, Mom."

Mom thought a minute and took a sip of her coffee. "No," she said. "I don't like the idea of me at work, far away, and you riding your bike who knows where."

"I want my bike!" I yelled.

"Not while I'm at work," Mom said, "and calm down."

I jumped to my feet so mad, my hands were shaking. *"Then why don't you quit your stupid job and stay home!"* I shouted. Then I spun around and ran out of the kitchen. I went into the bathroom, slamming the door behind me, and locked the door. Then I began to cry like a two-year-old baby.

Mom was knocking on the door. "Mark? Let me in."

I ignored her and put my face into a towel. I was miserable and low and lost and all for some stupid reason that didn't make any sense. I'd finally found a place for my bike and Mom wouldn't even listen to me.

"Mark," Mom called from outside the door. "Come on, sweetie."

It seemed to me that I cried for an hour, but it probably wasn't even five minutes. I washed my face and dried it with my towel. When I opened the door, Mom grabbed me in a hug. I tried to shake myself loose. "You're being unfair," I said.

"Then let's talk about it."

We walked back to the kitchen in silence and I sat down at the table. Mom poured me a glass of milk and set it before me.

"I don't understand you, Mark," she said. "Why is that bike so important?"

"It's very important," I said.

"But why?"

"I don't *know* why!" I said, louder than I wanted to. Mom looked at me from over her coffee cup. I took a sip of milk. "Look," I began again, "riding my bike is something I used to do and I want to do it again. . . ."

"Yes."

"Remember when I had nothing to do sometimes and I would just ride my bike around and around the block all afternoon?"

"I remember," Mom said.

"Well," I said, "most of the kids around here have bikes. And if I ever make some more friends, I could ride my bike over to their house."

"Mark . . ." Mom began.

"And maybe we could go riding together, like I used to do with Brett and Justin. And maybe some kid would have a hoop over the garage like we used to have. I miss that, too, Mom. I miss shooting a basketball and dribbling and fooling around on the court. I used to do that a lot. . . ."

"Honey," Mom said, but I found I had more to say.

"And maybe I'd find a friend who had a back porch like we used to and we could sit back there and play board games and stuff. Or we could throw a ball around, like Brett and Justin and I used to do. I miss that too. . . . So that's why I need my bike, Mom. It's like one thing I used to do that I could do again. And I really want it."

When I finished talking, Mom was staring at me with a sad look in her eyes. "Honey," she said, "yesterday is yesterday. You can't turn the clock back."

"I know that," I said. "But it looks like you won't let me go forward either. You and Dad . . . you do what you want, but I'm always stuck. Sometimes I feel like a football that you guys are tossing back and forth. Dad can see me only on Sunday, so that's what I have to do. You want me to run home from school and lock myself in this apartment. And what I want to do doesn't matter anymore."

Mom sighed and pushed the spoon around in her coffee cup. "Maybe that bike is more important than I thought," she said.

"It is," I said. "And I want it."

Mom said nothing for a while. I could hear the traffic outside and the refrigerator humming in the loud silence.

"Okay," she said. "But only if your father agrees."

20

HUNKY-DORY

I called my dad that night about getting my bike back. As soon as Mom went into the shower, I ran right into the kitchen and used the phone there. I have to admit I was being sneaky.

"Mom said it's okay," I told Dad. "You can bring my bike here anytime."

"Can I talk to her?"

"She's in the shower," I said, which was true. "Maybe we can get the bike on Sunday, when I see you. If you want, I can call Brett and make sure he'll be home."

"I suppose so," said Dad.

"And I need you to get a good lock for the storage-room door. With extra keys in case I lose one."

"Fine," said Dad. "You're sure all this is okay with your mother, now?"

"Of course," I said, stretching the truth again.

"Then I'll get your bike before Sunday," Dad said. "It probably needs to be cleaned up a bit. And I'm sure it can use a good oiling."

"I love you a thousand million times," I said to make Dad laugh, which he did.

"You sound different, Mark," Dad said. "Happy."

"Getting there," I said.

I was going to get my bike back. Next week I'd be riding that blue beauty all over the place. It felt good.

I told Joe about my bike the next morning, when we were on the way to school. "Maybe you can take an hour off and go bike riding with me."

"Bike riding's what I do every night," Joe said. "What's the big deal?"

"It's fun, Joe. Just zipping along seeing how fast you can go . . . cutting corners real tight and doing wheelies . . ."

"No, thanks," Joe said. "A bike's for business."

In class that day Jimmy Rossillo walked over to my desk and handed me the artwork he'd done for our report on the Sumerians. There were three drawings, each one terrific. "Wow," I told Jimmy, "you sure can draw."

"Well, of course," Jimmy said, like it was obvious. "Didn't you know I was the best?"

I walked to the Jade Garden with Joe after school. When we got to the back, we heard music coming from the little radio that sat on a shelf against the wall. And Mishi was holding her kitten against herself and dancing around.

"Look at that crazy kid," Joe said, not loud enough to stop Mishi from dancing. "Is she nutty, or what?"

Mrs. Chang and Uncle Han were sitting at the round table,

making dumplings. "Mark," Mrs. Chang said to me, "you ready for another lesson making dumplings?"

"Why not?" I went right off and washed my hands. But when I came back, I sat down next to Mrs. Chang and just watched her for a while instead of starting to make dumplings. I saw how she wet the outer edge of the round dough disk with a little paintbrush. How she put just the right amount of filling in the center of the disk. And I watched her fingers carefully, seeing how she bent the disk in a crescent-moon shape and exactly how she folded the edge to make a seal.

"I've got it," I said. I picked up a dough disk, filled it, and made a very good-looking dumpling . . . maybe not as good as Mrs. Chang's, but it was close.

"Very good, Mark," Mrs. Chang said as I did another.

"Thanks," I said. "Can I get a job here, making dumplings?"

Mrs. Chang laughed. "Yes, but you must join the family first."

"I thought I already had," I said, making her laugh again. I kept working until I had filled a dinner plate with dumplings.

One night later, when Mom and me went to the Jade Garden for dinner, we got a surprise. A few minutes after we sat down, and before we ordered our food, Mrs. Chang came out of the kitchen and set a plate of steamed dumplings down on our table.

"Helen," Mom said, "what's this?"

"Dumplings," said Mrs. Chang. "Mark made these yesterday."

Mom looked at me. "I didn't know you had such talent," she said.

117

"Eat them now," said Mrs. Chang, "before they get cold."
Guess what? I really liked those dumplings, even if I had made them myself. And so did Mom.

When we finished our dinner Mrs. Chang came back, and to my surprise she sat down and chatted with Mom for a long while. On the way home I asked Mom how come she and Mrs. Chang were so friendly.

"Because we speak now and then," Mom said.

"You do?" I said.

Mom laughed. "Sometimes I call from the office, checking up on you. And we chat. I don't tell you everything, young man," she said.

The next day I zipped right home after school and finished our report on the Sumerians. It looked great, with a beautiful cover made by Jimmy.

Mom came home exactly on time. "There's a letter for you, sir," she said as she put the mail on the table. I saw a pink envelope with my name and address on it. I picked it up and inspected it.

"Aren't you going to open it?" Mom asked.

"In a minute. I'm trying to think who could be writing me."

When I opened the envelope I got a surprise. It was an invitation to Libby Klein's birthday party.

Mom read the invitation over my shoulder. "How nice," she said. "Who's Libby Klein? I never heard you speak about her."

"She's a girl in my class."

"Why aren't you smiling?" Mom asked. "Is something wrong?"

"I'm very surprised, that's all. I hardly know Libby Klein."

"Well," said Mom, "she must like you."

"I'm not so sure about that," I said. "I think this is Carrie White's doing."

"Carrie White . . ." said Mom. "Oh, the girl who wants you to be her boyfriend."

"You got it."

Mom went off to change her clothes. I sat down at the kitchen table and stared at Libby's invitation. I really wanted to go to her party. Most of the kids in my class would be there. But on the other hand I didn't want a girlfriend, and especially not a ditzhead like Carrie White.

During dinner Mom said I had to telephone Libby to tell her if I was coming or not. "I'm going to go," I said, making up my mind. "What about a present?"

"We'll shop for it on Saturday. Maybe we'll go to the Grandview Mall and see what it's like."

After dinner I went to the telephone in Mom's room, where I could speak in private. I dialed Libby's number and then she was on the line. "Hi," I said, "it's Mark Baker. Thanks for inviting me to your party."

"No problem," said Libby. "I hope you're coming."

I hesitated for a couple of seconds. "Well," I said, "I guess I am. I mean, I am . . . but I have this problem with Carrie."

I heard Libby's little tinkly laugh. "Lots of boys have problems with Carrie."

"I know she's the reason you invited me," I said. "But I sure don't want to be her boyfriend."

"Then don't be."

"Right," I said. "But she doesn't seem to be the kind of girl who takes no for an answer."

"Just tell her to buzz off," said Libby. "In a nice way, of course."

"That's what I've been doing," I said. "She doesn't seem to hear me."

"Look, Mark, I've known Carrie since kindergarten. You just keep saying no and she'll find someone else."

"I hope you're right," I said.

"In fact," said Libby, "I think she already has her eyes on another boy."

"Who?"

There was Libby's laugh again. "Jimmy Rossillo."

"Jimmy? Really?"

"Really."

"But I haven't noticed anything," I said. "Are you sure?"

"Just watch who she sits down next to at lunch. Believe me, she's after Jimmy now."

"Whew," I said, letting out some air, "that's good news. Now I can go to your party without worrying about Carrie."

"Well," said Libby, "Carrie's not the only one who asked me to invite you to my party."

I didn't know what to say to that. I was surprised.

"Hello?" said Libby.

"Still here," I said. "Did you say someone else asked you to invite me? Who could that be?"

"That would be telling, wouldn't it?"

"Yeah," I said, "but I'd sure like to know who. I didn't think anyone in class even noticed me."

"You'd be surprised," said Libby.

"I am surprised. In fact, I'm amazed. Who asked you to invite me?"

"Well . . ." said Libby, pausing for a moment. "Promise never to tell them that I told you, okay?"

"Promise."

"Truly?"

"Truly," I said. "Up to the sky and down to the ocean."

Libby laughed again. "She'd kill me if she knew I told you. But . . . Joyce Appleman said you were the cutest thing and she wanted to make sure you were coming."

"Joyce Appleman?" I said. "She's the smartest girl in class, or one of them. But we've never even spoken to each other."

"Then there's Carrie, of course."

"Well, I know about Carrie," I said.

"And there's Linda Talbott and her friend, Misty Goldbloom."

"Linda and Misty?" I said. "But they talk only to each other. I never saw them look at me."

"Oh, they've noticed you, all right," said Libby. "And they'd like to know you better, especially Linda."

"I don't believe this," I said.

"I'll bet you didn't know you were so popular."

"Not in a million years."

"Linda and Misty," said Libby, "they've made a nickname for you. All the girls in class know it."

"I don't think I like this," I said. "What's the name?"

Libby was having a fit of giggles.

"Libby? Come on, tell me."

"I shouldn't," she said.

"Pretty please? With sugar on it. Tell me."

"Okay," she said, when she stopped giggling. "They call you 'The Incredible Hunk.' "

"What?"

"Now, that's all I'm going to say," said Libby, "because I've already told you too much. Except to say come hungry, because we're going to have lots of food. Okay?"

"Okay," I said, "and thanks." I hung up the phone and walked back to the kitchen. I still had trouble believing all that Libby had told me.

Mom looked at me. "Are you okay, babe?" she asked. "You look a little out of it."

"I'm fine," I said. "And I'm going to the party."

"Good."

"Except some girls are calling me 'hunk,' Mom. And I don't know whether I like that or not."

21
LIFE OF THE PARTY

Joe wasn't going to Libby's party, even though he was invited. That's what he told me the next day on the way to school. I asked him why.

"Saturday night is a busy time," he said. "Lots of orders to go."

"Couldn't you get one night off? So we could go together?"

"I could," said Joe, "but I won't. Besides, I already told Libby I couldn't come to her party."

I was beginning to wonder about Joe. It seemed like he did nothing but scoot home from school, play some chess, do his homework, and go to work. I wondered if he ever played ball or went to a movie or ever did anything just for the fun of it.

I was finishing my homework when I got a phone call from Minnie Olson. She asked me to come up and speak to her for a few minutes.

"It's the nosy old lady again," she said when she opened her door to me. "Come in."

I sat down on a chair in her kitchen.

"Tell me truthfully," she said, "have you seen Phil Stein-kraus the past few days?"

"No," I said. "I don't think he's been in school."

"How about after school?"

"Nope."

Minnie pursed her lips. "That's too bad," she said. "I was hoping you could clear up the mystery. His poor mother is worried sick."

"Why?"

"The school called her at work today. It seems that Phil has skipped school for three days and Hannah didn't know anything about it."

"I haven't seen him," I said. "And if I did, I'd walk the other way."

"That boy is a trial," Minnie said. "And he's headed for trouble."

On Saturday morning Mom and I left the house early to go to the Grandview Mall. All the way there in the car Mom chattered away about what I should wear and what we would do at Libby's party. I think she was more excited about me going to the party than I was.

What I was was nervous. I always get that way about parties, meeting new people, and going places I've never gone before.

We poked around the mall and went into Bowman's, the big department store. Mom found a fancy handkerchief she said was exactly right for Libby's present. I said a handkerchief was a dumb present. Why does a person need a fancy handkerchief when Kleenex does the job? Mom said something about being feminine and dressing up and she bought the handkerchief for Libby anyway.

We went to a card shop down the mall and I picked out a card for Libby myself, and not the one Mom thought was cute.

As soon as we got home Mom started right in again on what I was going to wear. Are all mothers so weird about how their kids should dress? Or is it only my mom? I hardly ever think about what I wear, but it's always on Mom's mind.

She laid out my good gray pants, a white shirt, my one and only tie, and the blue blazer that I'd worn to Aunt Edna's wedding a year ago. I sat on the edge of my bed and watched her. When she had it all together I just folded my arms, shook my head, and said, "No way I'm wearing that. It's too fancy."

"But you look so dreamy in that outfit."

"Dreamy? Mom, nobody wears a tie and a jacket to parties."

"Now, Mark," she said.

"I don't want to look like a goop."

"A goop?" said Mom. "What's that?"

"I don't know, but that's what I'll look like."

"Just try it on," she said in her you-better-obey voice.

I got off the bed and did what she said. The sleeves of the blazer were way too short and I could hardly button it.

"My goodness, you've grown," Mom said.

"Yeah," I said, a great big grin on my face. I knew I wasn't going to wear that blazer no matter what she said, but now we didn't have to fight about it.

I sat back down on my bed and watched as Mom went through my closet and my dresser. She took out all my good shirts and matched them up with my pants and sweaters. Once in a while she came over and held a sweater and shirt against my chest.

In the end we agreed I'd wear my gray pants, a blue shirt, and a plaid sweater.

Later, when I got dressed and came into the kitchen all ready to go, Mom inspected my face, my hands, and especially my fingernails. Then she made me go back and recomb my hair. "It's too long," she said, using her hand to push it down near my neck where it curls up a little. "You really should have gotten a haircut."

"Maybe I should have gone to Candy Steinkraus and had my nails done too," I said. I thought that was pretty funny, but Mom didn't.

I was all set to walk out the door when Mom insisted on driving me to Libby's house. "It's only six blocks away," I told her. "I'll walk."

"I'm driving you," she said, "and I'm going to pick you up after the party too."

"I can walk there and walk home," I protested. "I'm not a baby."

"Yes, you are," Mom said. "You're my one and only baby, and don't you forget it."

I was mad and I mumbled and grumbled, but Mom wasn't listening.

We pulled up in front of Libby's house. I got out of the car only to find that Mom was getting out too. "Mom, what are you doing?" I asked.

"I'm going to ask Mrs. Klein when I should pick you up."

"You're not coming in, are you?"

"Only for a minute," she said.

"Mom," I said, "please."

"Why ever not?" she said, and walked right past me to the door.

Before I could say anything more, the door opened and Mrs. Klein was standing there, smiling. "Hello," Mom said, "I'm Mark Baker's mother."

"How do you do," said Mrs. Klein.

I said hello to Mrs. Klein and walked inside, leaving Mom and Mrs. Klein talking. I'm glad none of the kids were there to see that my mom had actually brought me to the party.

Libby's house was bigger than our old one, and it had very high ceilings. I passed a table that had a few presents on it and I set my little box and card down among them.

I was going into the dining room just as Michael Marder was coming out. His face was all red and he looked really steamed. "Hi, Michael," I said, "what's up?"

"Steve Mayer," he said. "I hate that guy and I don't want to be anywhere near him. I'm going out to the backyard."

I followed Michael through the kitchen and out the back door. In the backyard there were lots of red and yellow lanterns hanging on the trees. A stereo was playing and kids were dancing. A man, Mr. Klein, I guess, was putting hot dogs on a barbecue grill.

The driveway was lit up by floodlights and kids were gathering there. As I walked over to join them, I heard the sound of a basketball bouncing on cement. I found Libby there. She was wearing a white dress and she looked really pretty. "Foul-shooting contest," she said. "Winner gets a present."

I said hello to Libby and then she turned around and called

someone over. Joyce Appleman came walking up to us. "Hi, Mark," she said. "I'm Joyce Appleman."

Joyce was wearing dark pants and a white sweater. Her dark hair was long and her teeth looked very white as she smiled at me. She stuck out her hand and we touched fingers for a second.

"Nice to meet you," I said to Joyce, "even though we've been in the same class for about a month."

Libby made us all get into a line in front of the basket. I walked with Joyce to the back of the line and we talked as we waited for our turn. Meanwhile kids in front of us stepped up to the foul line and tried to sink a basket. If you sank the shot you went back to the end of the line.

Joyce asked me how I liked the school and the neighborhood. She was very easy to talk to, and a good listener, and as we moved toward the front of the line I began to realize I wasn't nervous anymore.

Pretty soon we were up at the foul line. "I'm terrible at this," Joyce said to me. "I can hardly reach the basket."

"Try shooting underhand," I told her, and then I showed her how to do it.

"Next!" said Libby, after Marcy Lipton had shot an airball.

"Just keep your eyes on the front rim," I told Joyce as the ball came back to her. She took the ball in both hands, bent low, and came up and threw the ball high up on the garage roof way over the basket. Joyce started laughing. "I guess that was too strong, huh?"

"Just a little," I said.

Libby tossed the ball to me at the foul line. I took it in my hands and bounced it a few times. It felt really good, and I thought how long it'd been since I had a basketball in my hands. Back home I'd practiced shooting and dribbling around the court almost every day.

I aimed and took my one-handed shot and—*swish!*—the ball went through the hoop cleanly and settled in the cords.

"Nice shot," said Jimmy Rossillo, who was standing right behind me with Carrie.

I went back to the end of the line and Joyce came along to keep me company. When it was my turn again I hit another foul shot.

After a while there were only three kids in the contest: Jimmy, a quiet kid named Brian Perley, and myself. We each hit another two shots and then Brian shot and missed.

Everybody who was out had gathered around to watch us. Jimmy and I hit our next three shots and then Jimmy just bounced one off the rim and missed.

"Mark's the winner," Libby announced.

"One more try," I said, and Jimmy bounced the ball to me. I aimed and shot and the ball dropped through the hoop again.

"Don't you ever miss?" Joyce wanted to know.

"Let's see," I said as Jimmy fed me the ball. I hit another shot, then one more.

"That's ten in a row," Jimmy called. "The boy is hot as a pistol. Keep going, Mark."

I was beginning to feel like a show-off, and very, very lucky. I was a good foul shooter, but not this good.

"Last shot," I said. Then I covered my eyes with my left hand and shot the ball blind. Everybody yelled, including me, when the ball actually went in the hoop!

"Great shooting," Joyce said to me.

"Very lucky," I said. "I'm not this good."

"You should meet my brother, Quent," she said. "He's a basketball crazy."

Brian Perley said I could play basketball at his house anytime. And Jimmy wanted to make a date to play ball in the small park near his house.

When Libby yelled, "Time to eat," we all began walking over to the barbecue grill to get hot dogs and hamburgers. Then we picked up drinks and found places to sit down and eat. Joyce sat down next to me on the back-porch steps and Linda Talbott and Misty Goldbloom settled down right in front of us. Linda wanted to know all about where I used to live. I told her about our old house and the school I used to go to. Linda seemed nice, and also pretty with red hair and green eyes. Misty Goldbloom didn't say one word, but only listened.

When we all finished eating, Libby announced that it was time for some serious dancing. She turned up the stereo and we went down in the backyard and began dancing on the grass under the light of the colored lanterns.

Some kids don't like dancing, but I do. Maybe because I really know how. My mom likes to dance and she taught me.

I danced with Joyce for a while and then Linda. But it was so dark and crowded, it seemed like everyone was dancing with everyone. Libby came along and grabbed my arm and pulled me to the edge of the grass to dance with her. Except she really wanted to talk more than dance. "Having a good time?" she asked me.

"Sure am. This is a terrific party, Libby."

"Good," she said. "Will you do me a favor?"

"Sure."

"Would you go ask Misty Goldbloom to dance? She feels really bad that you've been dancing with Joyce and Linda and not with her."

"Okay," I said, "but why didn't Misty ask me to dance herself?"

"She's shy," said Libby, "which I'm not and you're not."

I thought about that for half a second. "But I really am shy," I said.

"You are?" said Libby. "You sure don't act like it."

"You're right," I said. "Maybe it's because I'm having a good time and all the kids seem friendly."

I found Misty Goldbloom standing by herself near the porch. "Hi," I said. "Want to dance?"

Misty nodded her head and we walked over to the grass. She had blond hair that sort of covered one side of her face and when she smiled she looked really nice.

We began dancing and neither of us said a word. I kept trying to think of things to ask Misty, but my mind was blank. I got the feeling Misty wanted to talk to me, too, but she didn't know what to say. When the music ended we just smiled at each other and waited for it to start again.

Later we all went inside and played some games, most of them silly. Then Libby's mom said it was time to open her presents. But before Libby did, she gave out prizes for all the winners of the games.

"For the best foul shooter . . ." Libby announced, and Jimmy yelled out, "Yeah, he's really foul." So everyone was laughing when Libby handed me a little Snoopy doll.

"Thanks," I said, "I always wanted to have a dog."

A little while later, after birthday cake, kids started going home. When I looked at my watch I saw it was almost mid-night. I couldn't believe the evening had gone so fast.

Mom showed up and stood at the front door talking with Mrs. Klein. Michael and Libby were standing together and I went over to say good-night. "Fantastic party," I told Libby.

"And you were a star," Libby said with a smile. "And thanks for dancing with you-know-who."

"Misty Goldbloom," Michael said with a grin.

"Never mind, birdbrain," said Libby.

I smiled all the way home in the car.

22

THE END OF HOPE

Instead of falling right asleep I lay in bed thinking about all the kids I'd gotten to know at the party. I could be friends with some of them.

It's funny how you make friends. I'd never given it much thought before. Back home I'd gotten to be best friends with Brett because we lived next door to each other. We started playing together when we were three and that was that. Then Justin moved in across the street and we got to be friends too.

I thought about the kids in my class and who was friends with who. Jimmy Rossillo was kind of a lone wolf, but he sometimes hung out with Michael and Libby. Libby was friends with everyone, especially all the girls, but she and Michael were friends. Ned Robbins and Steve Adolphus were best friends. Linda and Misty were a pair. Steve Mayer didn't have any friends except for Billy Alston, who was called his "shadow." Brian Perley used to be friends with Steve and Billy, but something had happened and he wasn't anymore.

THE SQUEAKY WHEEL

Phil Steinkraus was friends with no one because he didn't know how to be a friend. And I was friends with Joey Chang, but not yet best friends. Maybe that would come someday, if Joe ever got time off to ride a bike and shoot some hoops. Maybe he never would.

I guess I fell asleep after that, and when I woke up I knew it was late. My clock radio told me it was almost eleven o'clock in the morning. That's when I heard voices in the kitchen, speaking softly.

It was Mom and Dad!

I put my head back on the pillow and an old feeling came over me . . . like when I'd awaken back in our old house on a Sunday and I'd hear Mom and Dad talking in their bedroom across the hall. That always made me feel good, safe and sound in my own bed, with my folks nearby, and a whole day to be together in front of us.

I felt good now, and I got out of bed and into my slippers. I tiptoed into the hall to hear them better. Yes, it was Dad talking and Mom quietly laughing at something. No yelling, no screaming, no insults.

My wish was going to come true, I knew it. Mom and Dad would get back together and we'd be a family again. We'd move back into the house that belonged to us and life would be the same as it was before.

I stuck my face into the kitchen, followed by the rest of me. "Look who finally got out of bed," said Dad with a grin.

"Good morning, sleepyhead," said Mom.

"That must have been some party," said Dad.

I said good-morning and walked over to Dad, who gave me

a hug. "Get dressed," he said, "we've got big things to do today."

"Guess what?" said Mom with a big smile on her face.

Dad's coming back to live with us, I thought she was going to say next. I held my breath, waiting to hear it.

Instead, she said: "We've finally *sold* the house. Isn't that terrific?"

I looked at her, unable to speak. It was the end of all hope and all my silly dreams. I dashed from the kitchen and ran right to the bathroom, tears burning right behind my eyes.

The house was sold. It was gone. Dad and Mom and I would never live there again. New people would be moving in.

I turned on the cold water and put my head under the tap. *Wake up,* I told myself, dreaming time was over. I'd stay in this apartment with Mom. Dad was the guy I'd see on Sundays. *And this is your life, Mark Baker, like it or not.*

That's the bad part about getting your hopes up. When they come crashing to the ground you feel even worse.

I sat on my bed for a while. Then I began to get dressed, feeling low and moving slow. I wanted to get back into bed and cry, but I wouldn't let myself do it. *Hang tough. Right now.*

When I got back to the kitchen, Dad and Mom were talking about paying off the old mortgage. Mom was making notes on a yellow pad, adding up thousands of dollars. She looked so happy. "When's the closing?" she asked Dad.

"Couple of weeks," he said. "These people are in a hurry to get in there."

"It's great, Bill," she said.

Dad turned to me and said he had something for me downstairs.

"My bike," I said.

"Bingo," he said with a smile, and got to his feet.

We went downstairs, saying good-bye to Mom. The truck was parked around the corner on the side street. Dad climbed up into the bed of the truck, removed a tarp, and there it was. He lifted it and handed it down to me and I put my blue beauty onto the sidewalk.

Dad had cleaned it so it looked like new. "Thanks," I said.

Dad shot me a look. "I thought you'd be jumping in the air," he said.

I shrugged.

"Too much party last night, eh?" He jumped down from the truck and we went around the back of the house with the bike and down the ramp. I opened the door with my key and we put the bike into our storage space. Dad closed the door with a new padlock and handed me the keys.

My bike was back, but all the joy of it was spoiled.

That's how the rest of my Sunday with Dad went. He kept making jokes and being jolly to cheer me up, but it didn't help much. We drove to his apartment from the Hojo. It had started to rain. Dad hung shelves in his apartment. We watched about half a football game on TV and had sandwiches.

Later in the day we got into the truck in a heavy downpour and drove over to Trudy's house. Tiffany was standing beside her mother when she opened the front door. "Mock!" she said, all excited, when she saw me. She came right over and hugged my left knee.

"Looks like you made a friend," Dad said. When I glanced at him he was hugging Trudy.

I didn't want to see that, so when Tiffany tugged at my hand I followed her and we went off to the den to play. Mostly we sat on the floor and I rolled a tennis ball to her. She tried to catch it and laughed a lot when she didn't. It was a stupid game, perfect for this stupid day. Tiffany loved it.

Because it was raining so hard we didn't go out to dinner. Instead, Trudy had pizza delivered and we ate it in the kitchen. I don't think I said ten words during dinner. I chewed my pizza and drank my soda. Dad and Trudy were having a great time, joking around and laughing while they ate.

I said good-bye to Trudy and Tiffany after dinner and Dad and I dashed through the rain to the pickup. "It's coming down in buckets," Dad said when we were inside the cab. "Hope it keeps up."

"Why do you want it to keep up?" I asked.

"Because then it won't come down," he said, slapping a big hand on my knee.

I nodded.

"That's all?" he said. "Not even a smile for one of my best jokes?"

We drove back slowly, Dad watching the road shiny in the rain. He put the radio on and hummed along with the music as the windshield wipers tried to keep time. I didn't say anything. When we got near home, Dad asked if I was getting sick.

"Nope."

"Something bothering you, then?"

I shrugged.

THE SQUEAKY WHEEL

"Mark," he said, "you've been moping around all day. What's wrong?"

I watched the windshield wipers beating back and forth. "The same old thing," I said. "You and me and Mom."

Dad pulled to a stop in front of our apartment house.

"You've got to let it go," he said, "make your peace with it."

"Yeah, I know."

"You can't let it keep eating you up, babe," he said.

I had lots of things to say, but they just hung up in my throat like a lump. "It's hard," I said, "it's very hard."

Dad patted my knee then, and kissed the top of my head.

"Thanks for my bike," I said. Then I got out of the truck and dashed through the rain to my door.

23

RAINY DAYS AND SUNDAYS

It was another horrible Sunday night.

I lay in my bed in the dark, listening to the rain plonking down on my windowsill. I wanted to sleep but I couldn't shut off my mind. I'd close my eyes and all of a sudden I was thinking about this morning . . . hearing Mom and Dad talking so peaceably in the kitchen.

It was dumb of me to think they were going to get back together.

I thought about Trudy and Tiffany, and how it looked like my Sundays were always going to include them. I didn't hate Trudy or Tiff. But why should I have to share my dad with them every Sunday? I had only one day with him, and I wanted every minute of it for myself.

I closed my eyes again and saw Dad and Trudy hugging at her front door. Dad was going to marry her, I knew it.

I sat up and looked at my clock radio. It was 12:09 and it was Monday morning now.

THE SQUEAKY WHEEL

I got out of bed and walked over to the window. There were puddles in the backyard and dimples of rain smacking into them.

It was Dad, I thought, it was all about Dad. I wanted him all for myself and at the same time I could see him moving away from me. He was leaving my life, getting away from me and closer to Trudy. It hurt.

Back in the old days, even when things were good, even then I wanted more of him. I remembered that feeling.

I'd see Dad every morning. He'd be sitting in his chair at the table drinking coffee when I came downstairs for breakfast. He always gave me a smile and a hello to start the day. I loved seeing him there, his name stitched in script over the pocket of his work-shirt. He left for work then, before I had breakfast, and I always thought he didn't leave until he'd said good-morning to me.

I missed him so much at night. I remember how I'd always drop what I was doing when his pickup came rolling up the driveway. If I was playing outside I'd run to him. If I was inside I'd dash to the door so he could grab me up in his arms.

At the dinner table he'd always ask me what had happened in school that day. And he'd listen to what I had to say, making jokes sometimes, but always interested in me and my day.

Weekends were the best, and holidays. Any day that Dad was home and we were all together. I loved helping him do things around the house. I loved when he taught me about tools, especially the ones he worked with. I could use a wire stripper, holding it not too tight or too loose to pull a piece of insulation off the end of a wire. I could handle a screwdriver, a wrench, a pair of pliers. When Dad was up on a ladder working he could just call down to me: "Hand me a needle-nose, Mark," and I'd pick it right out of his toolbox and pass it to him. I loved that, being Dad's helper. It made me feel special.

I could spend hours hanging around with him, doing nothing, or watching a ball game on TV. He taught me all about sports, threw a ball to me until I could catch it, then threw and threw until I could hit it with my Wiffle bat. He showed me how to shoot baskets and dribble a basketball, and he let me win a lot of times when we played in the driveway.

I loved raking leaves with him in the fall, shoveling snow with him in the winter. Mom would make hot chocolate for us when we came in from the cold. "My two workingmen," she'd say, and I remember how that made me feel good.

Now he was slipping away from me week by week, and it hurt. There wasn't enough Dad in my life anymore. That's why I walked around being so sad. Not enough Dad.

It was like there was a part of me missing and it was in another town in another house and I got it back only for a short time on Sundays.

Whoever invented divorce never thought about kids. Parents split away from each other to make themselves happy. But all the happiness they get is taken right out of their kids.

Now I was always on a seesaw. One minute up, then back on the ground again. And always a part of me missing Dad.

I was so happy about getting my bike back again. Now it was down in the storage room waiting for me and I didn't even care about it.

Not enough Dad.

I climbed back into bed and twisted the covers around me. I knew I was nowhere near sleep.

THE SQUEAKY WHEEL

Maybe I could telephone Dad this week and maybe he'd even be there to answer the phone. *Dad,* I could say, *how about you pick me up on Friday night and we could spend the whole weekend together?*

I work on Saturdays, remember? he'd say.

Well, I could say, *I'll be your helper. I'll go with you on a job and hand you tools and things and I'd be sure to stay out of your way, I promise.*

He'd probably say no to that.

I could write Dad a letter. *Dear Dad, I miss you a lot all week long. Could you maybe just come over a couple of nights and hang around with me until I go to bed?*

That was dumb. And I knew Mom wouldn't allow it.

What could I do?

I could speak up at least and tell him we didn't have to see Trudy and Tiffany every Sunday night. I could certainly do that. But what if it made Dad disappointed in me? He probably would be. And he might even get angry with me.

I never wanted to do that.

The squeaky wheel gets the grease. Right. If I wanted something from Dad I had to ask for it. He wasn't a mind-reader. I had to speak up.

Why did that scare me so much?

24
INVASION OF THE GIRLS

Once it started raining it seemed like it would never stop. All that week it rained so often, I never even took my bike out of the storage room.

I walked to school in the rain with Joe and told him all about Libby's party. He couldn't believe I'd made so many foul shots in a row. "Are you really that good?" he asked.

"Good and lucky."

"I stink in basketball," Joe said. "Most other sports as well."

"How could you be good? You never even play ball."

"Even if I played," said Joe, "I probably would stink."

"You should have come to Libby's party," I said. "I'm sure your folks would have given you a night off if you'd asked for it."

"Don't start that again," Joe said.

"The squeaky wheel gets the grease, Joe. But I think you're too chicken to ask for time off. I think you're afraid."

"I am not."

"Yes, you are," I said. "You'd rather run home and lock yourself up in the restaurant. Never play ball, never go to a party, never have any fun. And never have any friends except me."

"Why are you mad at me?" Joe asked.

"I'm not mad at you," I said. "I'm mad at the whole stupid world."

Joe stopped walking and I did too. We stood under a tree in the rain, getting wet.

"I like you teaching me chess," I said. "But I could teach you basketball. Wouldn't that be good?"

"You know I don't have time, Mark."

"You could have time, if you ever asked your folks for it."

"Just leave my family out of this," Joe said. He glared at me with angry eyes from under the bill of his baseball cap. "My family means more to me than anything else, got that?"

"Even friends?"

"Yes," said Joe, "even friends."

"Even me?"

Joe's mouth softened, then widened into a grin. "I'll make an exception in your case. But only because Mom treats you like one of the family."

We let it go at that and walked on to school.

Mr. Pangalos gave us back our reports on the Sumerians. Carrie, Jimmy, and I got an A— for our report. Mostly because I made a few spelling errors, which were marked in red pencil.

Now we were beginning two months of work on ancient Egypt. It meant we would have to form committees again and make another big report. But this time Mr. Pangalos said we could form our own committees, which got a loud cheer from the class. "Do I hear a murmur of approval?" Mr. Pangalos said with a smile. "Okay, you've got ten minutes to get organized."

Joe popped up from his seat and came back to my desk in the back of the room. "So it'll be you and me and someone else," he said.

"Right," I said.

We stood there looking around the room, figuring out who we would like to ask to be the third member of our committee. That's when the invasion of the girls began.

Marcy Lipton came over to Joe and me. "Mark," she said, "can I get you on my committee?"

This was truly amazing, because Marcy Lipton had never spoken to me before.

"Well," I said, "Joe and I are working together. All we need is one more person."

"But I already told Nancy Moriarty that I'm working with her," said Marcy.

"Then we can't get together," I said.

As soon as Marcy turned away, Linda Talbott came along. "Mark," she said, "I want you on my committee. We need only one more."

"So do we," I said.

"Who's we?" asked Linda.

"Me and Joe."

A frown crossed Linda's face. "I'm working with Misty," she said. I could almost see Linda's mind working. "But maybe I'd rather work with you guys." Linda turned around and scooted across the room to talk to Misty Goldbloom.

That's when Joyce Appleman showed up. "I'm looking for someone to work with," she said.

Alongside Joyce, Joe was nodding his head up and down to me. Joyce was the smartest girl in the class, and everyone knew it.

"Joe and I need one more," I said. "You could join us if you like."

"I like," said Joyce.

"Me too," said Joe.

We stood talking about who would do what and where we'd meet to begin working. Joyce said the only fair way was to take turns meeting at each other's houses.

"That's fine with me," I said. "But I don't know about Joe. He always likes to work at his place."

"I'll work anywhere," Joe said. "As long as I get back home by five o'clock."

"What if we have to work a little longer?" Joyce asked.

Joe hesitated for a moment, thinking it over. "I really have to get to work on time," he said.

I kept thinking about Joe all afternoon. Did his folks really keep him working all the time? Or was part of it Joe's doing?

Joe had other things on his mind when we walked home from school. "How did you get so popular?" he wanted to know.

"I told you," I said. "You should have gone to Libby's party."

"All the girls are after you," Joe said in a teasing way.

"This is true," I admitted. "Probably because of my charm and the fact that I'm incredibly handsome."

Joe whooped out loud.

"Just call me hunk," I said.

That's when Joe punched me on the arm and I ended up chasing him through the rain, all the way back to the Jade Garden.

25

THIS WAY LEADS TO HAPPINESS

Mrs. Chang was sitting at the family table, writing in a big checkbook, when Joe and I came in all wet and drippy. "My two best boys," she said, then took off her eyeglasses and got a closer look at us. "Best very wet boys," she added.

"It's raining cats and dogs," I said.

"Frogs too," said Joe. "Even turtles and newts."

Mrs. Chang spoke to Joe in Chinese and he complained, "Oh, Ma!"

"Do it," said Mrs. Chang. "And bring dry socks for Mark."

"Mom wants me to change into dry clothes," Joe said to me. "I have to go upstairs to our apartment." He headed for the front door.

"Sit down," Mrs. Chang told me. "Take off your sneakers and socks. Wet feet make you sick." She went off to the kitchen and came back with a towel.

I took off my wet stuff and dried my feet with the towel.

Mrs. Chang disappeared into the kitchen, and when she came back she carried a tray with cups and a pot of hot tea.

"Joe missed a terrific party last Saturday night," I told her.

"Drink your tea," she replied. She poured a cup of tea for me and watched while I took a sip. "What party?"

"It was a birthday party for a girl in our class," I said. "Everyone was there. I know Joe was invited, but he didn't go."

"Joe said nothing about a party," she said.

"That's Joe," I said. "Maybe he was afraid."

"My Joe . . . afraid?" said Mrs. Chang, her eyebrows rising.

"I think so."

"Afraid of what?" she asked me.

I took a small sip of tea. "Of you," I said.

"Joe afraid of me?" said Mrs. Chang. "But why?"

"I think he's afraid to ask for time off," I said. "Joe says the family business comes first."

Mrs. Chang's small mouth came together to make an O. "This is true?"

"I think so."

Mrs. Chang pulled the checkbook toward her and put her glasses on. "Why didn't Joe say anything about this party to me?"

I shrugged.

"Foolish child," said Mrs. Chang. "Deliveries are not so important."

"Joe says they are," I said.

"Business is important, yes," said Mrs. Chang. "But Han can make deliveries. This he did when Joe was sick."

"Joe thinks he has to work all the time."

"Not so."

"But that's what Joe *thinks,*" I said. "And what he does."

Mrs. Chang stared off toward the front door for a moment. "This is as you say," she said. "Joe likes to help and be good. But Joe must also do what other boys do. He is only young for a short time."

"That's what I think," I said.

Mrs. Chang smiled at me and reached out a hand to brush some wet hair off my forehead. "You're a good friend to my Joe," she said. "First friend and best friend."

"Joe's my best friend too," I said.

"I will talk to Joe," she said.

I took a sip of my tea, watching Mrs. Chang. Her face looked sad to me.

"When a child does not speak," she said, "how are parents to know what makes a child unhappy? Parents must talk to children and children must always talk to parents. This way leads to happiness."

I nodded at what Mrs. Chang said, and even as I did that a thought came clear in my mind. I had some talking of my own to do about what was making me unhappy. I had to talk to my dad.

Joe was very cold to me as we walked to school the next morning. He wouldn't even look me in the eye. "Did I ask you to talk to my mother?" he asked me after a while.

"No."

"Then why did you butt in?"

"It just came up," I lied. "I told her about Libby's party and how you missed it."

"She was very mad at me, for your information," said Joe.
"I'm sorry."

"You should be," said Joe. "You went behind my back."

"Yeah," I admitted, "I did. And what happened?"

"You don't want to know," Joe said. "A one-hour lecture."

"Uh-oh."

"Even my *father* got involved," Joe said. "And he started
with his lawyer business again. He wants me to go to college
and then to law school. I don't know why he thinks being a
lawyer is so great. It sounds pretty boring to me."

"How about your mom?"

"She's hard to figure out sometimes," Joe said. "You know
how she's always telling me that Chinese things are so great?
Now she says I have to be a real American and do more things
like other kids do."

"Like what?"

"Go to parties," Joe said, "that's one thing."

I couldn't help smiling. "Is that so tough?" I asked.

Joe's serious face broke into a grin. "I guess not."

"And are we still friends?" I asked.

"Only just," said Joe, tapping me lightly on the arm.

"The squeaky wheel gets the grease," I said. "It's true."

"Yeah," said Joe. "Only next time, let *me* do the squeaking,
okay?"

26
CLOSING

Mom had to take an afternoon off from work. She told me she and Dad had to go to a closing on our old house. A closing, she explained to me, was when the official sale of a house takes place. There are lawyers for the buyer and the seller, and all sorts of papers are exchanged.

So now the house was officially gone. It saddened me some when I thought about it, but Mom came breezing in like she'd just won the lottery. "We did it!" she exclaimed, and she threw her arms around me and gave me a huge hug and too many kisses.

"Pardon me if I don't get excited," I said when I'd broken loose from her. "I loved that house, Mom. And I wish we were still living there."

"I understand that," she said. "But, Mark, this is your whole future. And mine."

"What is?"

"Selling the house, you goose! The money! Don't you understand that now we have some security? You can go to college, and I can even change my job without worrying about how we'll manage."

There was no stopping Mom's happiness. She threw together a pickup dinner, singing while she worked. It looked like she couldn't stop smiling.

When she was drinking coffee I asked her about something that was on my mind. I said it carefully, so she wouldn't get too mad at me. "Do you think, Mom, that maybe—just for once—you could cook dinner and invite Dad over to eat with us?"

Mom's whole face tightened up like a fist. "Absolutely not."

"Why not? Just once."

"Don't be ridiculous," she said. "I'm sure you've noticed that your dad and I don't get along too well right now."

"I've noticed," I said, trying to make it a joke.

"The less time we spend together, the better," she said.

"One time? One night?" I said. "You could do it."

"I have cooked my last meal for Bill Baker," Mom said. "You can go to the bank with that."

"Okay," I said, "but how about if we all went out to dinner?"

"Forget about it" is what she said.

I went to the freezer and took out some ice cream. Mom sipped her coffee, watching me. I scooped some ice cream into a small bowl and brought it back to the table.

"I want to understand this," I said. "You're saying that you and me and Dad are *never* going to be together? Is that it?"

"Oh, honey," Mom said. "You look like a poor lost puppy dog."

"Yeah," I said, "that's how I feel."

"I'm sorry, Mark, but I can't see your dad and me spending more than five minutes together. It's just the way things are."

"You really hate each other, don't you?" I stared at Mom, waiting for an answer.

After a while she spoke. "We don't hate each other, not exactly. But there's a lot of anger and sorrow and hurt between us. When we get together . . . it's sort of like opening a sore that's barely had time to heal. It's going to take time for those feelings to go away."

"How much time?" I asked.

"I don't know," she said with a shrug.

"Years and years?"

"I hope not," she said. "I know how much you love your dad. He has a lot of fine qualities, even if I can't stand the sight of him right now."

I squished the ice cream around in the bowl to help it melt. "What's going to happen when I graduate from school? Will one of you not come?"

"Don't be silly," Mom said.

"I don't think that's silly," I said.

"We'll both be there," Mom said. "But perhaps we won't sit together."

"And what about my birthday?" I said.

"I'll worry about that next February," Mom said.

"But will Dad be there?"

Mom made a face and rolled her eyes. "Mark, I just don't know."

"How about Christmas?"

"We'll try to make it a good one, honey," Mom said.

"Who?"

"The two of us together."

"You mean you and Dad?" I asked.

Mom shook her head. "No. Just you and me."

"Swell," I said in a sarcastic way. "And what about Thanks-giving?"

"I haven't thought about it," she said.

"Well, maybe you should," I said. "Will you invite Aunt Edna and her new husband again?"

"His name is Henry," Mom said. "And I certainly won't."

"Why not?"

"Because Aunt Edna is your dad's sister, that's why. And she hasn't said one word to me since she heard about the divorce."

"So who's coming for Thanksgiving?" I asked.

"Mark! Lay off!" Mom said in a loud voice.

"Nobody's coming, right?"

"Look," Mom said, "it's going to be just you and me. And we'll do the best we can, okay?"

"And you won't invite Dad. Not even for one day."

"Sorry," Mom said. "That I won't do."

Maybe I was getting used to disappointment by now, but I didn't even think of crying. It was just that seesaw again, and now I was down. "Tell you what," I said, "maybe we should just pretend there is no Thanksgiving this year. I'll pretend school is open and I'll go there. You get dressed and go to work . . ."

"Mark . . ."

THE SQUEAKY WHEEL

"How can you have Thanksgiving," I said, "when you have nothing to be thankful for?"

I got up, took my melted bowl of ice cream, and set it in the sink. And I didn't say one word to Mom the rest of the night.

27

$\mathcal{A}$T THE MALL

It turned out that we did most of our Egypt-committee work at Joyce Appleman's house, even though she was the one who'd said we should take turns. Joyce's house was close to school and she liked having Joe and me there. So twice a week we began walking home from school with her.

Our report was on the kids of ancient Egypt. It wasn't easy to get information on what a kid's life was like in those olden days. We used Joyce's encyclopedia, but there really wasn't much in it. One day we all went to the library on Cortelyou Road. There was a nice librarian there, Stacy, and she found two books for us—one was a novel—that told us what we needed to know.

Kids in ancient Egypt weren't too bad off, because Egyptians had a good family life and loved their kids. Boys mainly learned their fathers' trades. But only the royal boy kids were taught to read and write, not girls. Girls stayed home and were taught cooking and other things by their mothers.

157

We didn't find anything about divorce back then, so maybe there wasn't any.

In between the work we did on our report, we managed to have a lot of fun at Joyce's house. She has an older brother, Quentin, and he's a basketball freak. He always wanted to get us out on the court in the driveway near the garage. We played two against two, mostly, Joe and me against Quent and Joyce. Joyce was terrible, and Joe was hardly better, but it was still fun.

Joe wasn't in such a great hurry to get home now. And he didn't have to work delivering orders every night. Han was doing some of that.

I was beginning to like Joyce a lot. She really was very nice, in addition to being so smart.

In school the three of us became a trio. Joyce and Joe and I had lunch together almost every day. One day Joyce suggested that the three of us go to the Grandview Mall on Saturday.

I thought Joe would surely say no, but when Joyce said we would hang out, have lunch, and then see a movie he said okay.

"You're sure you won't change your mind?" I asked him. "At the last minute?"

"Joe won't do that," Joyce said as Joe poked me under the table.

There was a bus that went directly to the mall from town and it stopped right in front of the A & P. We planned to meet there at the bus stop.

Joe rang my doorbell that Saturday and we went across the street to wait for Joyce. A little while later, to our surprise, a car pulled up driven by Mrs. Appleman. Joyce poked her head out the passenger-side window. "Hop in," she said. "We're getting a lift to the mall."

Joe and I got into the backseat and the car pulled away. "Thanks very much," Joe said to Mrs. Appleman. Joyce turned around and made a face at us. I could see she wasn't happy.

We all went into the mall entrance together, then Mrs. Appleman said she had some shopping to do and walked off toward the department store. The minute she left, Joyce started trashing her mom.

"She treats me like a baby," she said. "As if I'd die if I took the bus here with you guys."

"Getting a ride was nice," I said.

"Right," said Joe. "We saved the bus fare, didn't we?"

We went into the hamburger place and found an empty table. As we were eating, Joyce talked about her mom. "She didn't have any shopping to do," Joyce said. "She just came along to make sure we got here safely. She watches me like a hawk. And I'm getting sick of it."

"How about if she didn't care?" Joe asked. "Wouldn't that be worse?"

"You don't understand," Joyce said.

By the time we finished eating, Joyce had calmed down and was her usual self. We left and went into the card shop to look around. After that we went to Steve's and got ice cream cones. We had about fifteen minutes before our movie started. It was at the other end of the mall and we began walking that way.

We came around a bend in the mall and there was a mob of people. It wasn't just the usual crowded mall; these people weren't moving. We had to kind of push and wriggle our way through them. "What's going on?" Joyce asked a woman in front of us.

"They caught some kid shoplifting," she said.

Joe led Joyce by the hand and I followed as we snaked through the crowd of people. What we saw as we got to the front stopped us. There was Phil Steinkraus, up against the wall, and two security guards were holding him.

"Walked out of that store with a camouflage jacket," a man behind us said.

"Without paying for it," another man said, then laughed. "He'll pay for it now."

Phil Steinkraus had his Mr. Cool face on and his hands behind his back. He kept staring people in the eye, his chin up. In a moment he saw my face. "Hey, Marky," he called out to me, "how ya doin'?"

One of the security guards turned around and looked me over. "Son," he said, "don't come any closer and don't do anything funny."

"Let's get out of here," Joyce whispered, and Joe took a step across the cleared circle and toward the movies. But I just couldn't believe what I was seeing. And my feet refused to move.

Phil turned his body to show me why he had his hands behind his back. He had handcuffs on. "I told these guys I had money to pay for it, Marky," he said.

"Then why didn't you?" the taller of the two guards said.

"It's all a mistake," Phil said.

"Yeah," said the guard, taking Phil's arm, "yours, kid." He and the other guard began walking Phil away from us as people made room for them to pass.

Without thinking about it I began to follow them, and Joyce and Joe fell in behind me.

"Where are we going?" I heard Phil ask.

"Outside," said the tall guard. "The police will meet us there."

Phil and the two guards came to a flight of steps that led to the lower level of the mall and the parking lot. Phil twisted his head around toward me. "Marky," he said, "will you call my mom?"

"Okay," I said. "Where is she?"

"At work," Phil said as they began walking him down the stairs.

I stood at the top of the stairs, Joyce and Joe right behind me, and watched until Phil and the guards were downstairs and out of sight.

"We're going to miss our movie," Joyce said.

"That's right," Joe said.

"You heard him," I said. "I've got to call Phil's mom."

No one said anything for a moment. Then Joe said, "I really hate Phil Steinkraus."

"Me too," said Joyce.

"Everyone hates him," I said. "But I'm still going to call his mother."

No one said a word, but we all turned and began walking toward the wing of the mall where the telephones were. I didn't have a quarter, so Joe handed me one from his pocket. I called information and they gave me the number of the A & P on Beverly Road.

I dialed the number and a man answered. "I have to talk to Hannah Steinkraus," I told him.

"She's working the checkout," the man said. "Is this Phil?"

"No," I said, "but I have to talk to her right now. It's really important."

The man grumbled a moment, then told me to hang on. I waited a long time, enough for the telephone voice to come on and ask for another quarter. "Another quarter," I said, and Joe dug into his pocket and handed it to me.

"That's fifty cents you owe me," Joe said.

Then Mrs. Steinkraus was on the phone. I told her who I was. "Phil just got arrested for shoplifting at the Grandview Mall," I said. "The cops are taking him away."

I really expected Mrs. Steinkraus to start yelling, or crying, or both. But all she did was sigh. "That boy," she said. "Thanks. I'll have to get him out."

Then we hung up the telephone.

The three of us walked to the movies after that, but the film we'd wanted to see had already started. We decided to see a different one, and I got change when I bought my ticket. I gave Joe back his fifty cents.

All through the movie, a dumb comedy, I kept thinking about Phil Steinkraus. I kept remembering how he looked in handcuffs, walking down those stairs between two guards. I had the feeling I'd never forget it.

Phil was probably right about me. I was just another one-dollar friend. Maybe less. Now I was just a fifty-cent friend.

28

S UNDAY SHOWDOWN

This was going to be the Sunday I'd talk to Dad. If I was ever going to see more of him, I had to do it.

Dad showed up a little earlier than usual, before I was all dressed. I heard his voice in the kitchen, talking to Mom. I buttoned my shirt quickly, threw a sweater on, and went out to get my hug.

"Better wear a warm jacket," he said, "it's getting nippy out there."

I did that, then kissed Mom good-bye, and we went down-stairs and into the pickup.

We didn't say much as we drove along. It was a clear day with the sun peeking out now and then from behind fast-moving gray clouds. Most of the trees were bare, and brown leaves were blowing in the wind. It reminded me of other Sundays in the fall when I'd be outside on the lawn with Dad.

Leaf-time was always a combination of work and fun. Dad would be using the old bamboo rake, scraping around the lawn and gathering leaves. He'd put them into a pile that grew bigger and bigger until it was high enough for me to land on top of it in a flying leap. After that I'd hold open the big plastic bag while Dad filled it with the dead brown leaves.

We got off at Dad's exit and started heading for the Hojo. "I'm ready to tear into breakfast," Dad said. "This weather gives me an appetite."

"Could we skip the Hojo?" I asked him.

"Sure. You got a hankering for some other place?"

"No," I said. "I'm just tired of always eating in the same place."

"Whatever you say." He drove past the Hojo and we got onto a road lined with gas stations, stores, and restaurants. "Franchise heaven," said Dad. "When you see a place you like, sing out."

We went past a Sizzler, Denny's, Burger King, and McDonald's. Up ahead I saw a blue roof. "How about the I Hop?" I said.

"Okey-dokey," said Dad.

He turned into the parking lot and we went inside. A hostess seated us at a table in the middle of the place, then gave us menus. Then a waitress came over and poured coffee for Dad. She went away and we studied our menus.

"What'll it be?" asked Dad.

"I don't know. I'm not too hungry."

Dad looked at me over the top of his menu. "I sure hope you're in the mood for pancakes," he said. "Or else, why are we here?"

I ordered the apple pancakes when the waitress came back. Dad wanted wheatcakes with bacon, plus a side order of sausage patties. When the food came, Dad attacked it—he really was hungry—and he finished everything on his plate and what I left on mine.

He lit his cigarette and got his coffee cup refilled by the waitress. "Not much appetite this morning, babe," he said. "You feeling all right?"

"Fine."

"Coming down with something, are you?"

"Nope."

Dad took a long sip of coffee, then puffed on his cigarette. Blue smoke curled up in front of his face. "You seem awfully quiet this morning, Mark. You got something on your mind?"

"Yes," I said, getting even more nervous than I already was.

"I thought so," Dad said. "What's bothering you?"

I took a deep breath and held it. "You are," I said.

"Uh-oh," Dad said, shooting me a grin. "I may be in big trouble here."

"I don't want to see Trudy and Tiffany anymore," I said. "And especially not on Sunday, the one measly day I get to spend with you."

Dad's eyes blinked a few times and he turned his head away from me. I could hear my heart beating.

"I see," said Dad. "Any particular reason?"

"Yes," I said. "They're not my family and you are. And even if you marry Trudy, she won't be my family."

"Whoa, there," said Dad, "slow down."

"I wait all week for the one day I get to spend with you. But I miss you every single day."

"And I miss you too," said Dad.

"No, you don't," I said. "You never call me on the telephone. I'm always calling you and you're always out and I end up leaving you a message on your stupid machine. Why don't you ever call me back?"

"I do," Dad said.

"No, you don't."

"I call back, Mark, but you're usually asleep."

"Then why don't you call back the next day? In the morning, before I go to school. Or at night. You know the time we have dinner, don't you?"

"Okay, okay," Dad said, his cheeks starting to get pink.

"It's not okay," I said. "You're divorcing Mom. And you know what? I think you want to divorce me too."

The corners of Dad's mouth sagged when I said that. "That's unfair, Mark," he said.

"I don't care a rat's toenail if it's unfair," I said, "that's the way I feel. I used to see you every single day and now I hardly see you at all. And I have this horrible feeling that you want to get out of my life. I can feel you sliding away from me and I don't know why you want to do that," I said, my voice getting louder and people around us starting to look over at us.

"Pipe down," Dad said.

"I hate what's happening," I said. "I hate playing with Tiffany while you spend time with Trudy. And when we go out you talk with Trudy and I'm supposed to talk to Tiff."

"She likes you, Mark," Dad said.

"Who cares if she likes me?" I said. "You're the one who's my father, not her."

"Shhh," Dad hissed at me, "quiet."

"You're the one I want to see, not anybody else. I know you're going to marry Trudy, don't deny it. And I know what's going to happen after that. You'll see Tiff every day, not me. I'll be just a Sunday visitor to you, like I already am. Not your son that you used to hug every single day."

"Stop it!" Dad said in a loud voice. "Just shut up for a minute and let's get out of here." He jumped up fast and knocked his chair back, fished in his pocket for money, and threw some bills down on the table. Then he spun around and started walking really fast toward the door, not waiting for me, and for one awful moment I thought Dad was running away and leaving me there.

I jumped up and started to follow, then remembered my jacket. I went back to get it and ran after him. He was outside and heading for the pickup when I caught up.

"Get in the damn truck," Dad barked at me.

I ran around the pickup to the passenger side as Dad jumped into the truck and gunned the engine, then I climbed in. Dad spun the wheels and pulled out of the parking lot in a hurry. I knew he was awfully angry with me.

"You just embarrassed the hell out of me," Dad said. "I hope you enjoyed it."

I swallowed the lump in my throat.

Dad was driving like a maniac, passing cars right and left, going way too fast. He kept his eyes glued to the road, his hands gripping the steering wheel really tight.

"I'm sorry," I managed to say, but Dad didn't take his eyes off the road. I was really scared. "Dad," I said, "I got excited. I'm really sorry."

There was a red light ahead and Dad hit the brakes and we came to a squealing stop. He still didn't say one word or even glance over at me.

THE SQUEAKY WHEEL

We waited what seemed like a long time for the light to turn green. When it did, Dad shot away from the light.

"I didn't mean to make you mad at me, Dad. I'm . . . sorry. I just—I just don't want you to leave me . . . and I think you're going to."

Dad made a strange sound then, a kind of moan down deep in his throat, and he hit the brakes and pulled the pickup to the shoulder of the road and finally stopped it. Then he put his face in his hands and leaned down low on the steering wheel.

He was crying! My father was crying, I could hardly believe it. It made me feel so sad.

I reached over and put my hand on his shoulder and in a second he turned and grabbed me in a hug. "Baby, baby," he sobbed in a broken voice, "I'm so sorry."

We stayed that way for a time in the cab of the pickup; Dad holding on to me real tight, crying a lot, cars passing by outside, the traffic lights ahead clicking as they turned from red to green and back again.

In a little while Dad got out his hankie and wiped his eyes. He smiled at me as he put his hankie away, then cleared his throat. "If you think I haven't been lonely, you're very wrong," he said.

Dad ran the back of his hand across his eyes. "I do miss you, Mark. Miss seeing you when I come home, miss hearing about all your adventures in school. Somewhere in the middle of all this fussing and fighting with your mom . . . I think I almost lost you, boy."

Dad's hand came up and smoothed the top of my hair.

"I've been in a bad way since I left," he said. "But I want you to remember this: You're my son forever and ever and I'm not going to let you slip away from me, hear?" Dad put the truck in gear and slowly pulled off the shoulder and back onto the road. "I'm not too good at being a long-distance father," he said. "I know I'll have to work at it."

"We have to be together more," I said.

"That's for sure," he said. "It's been lonely for me, too, babe. And I hate being cooped up in that tiny place. Can't stand it sometimes . . . like the walls are closing in on me. I just get up and run away . . . to the movies, bowling, anything. I think that's how I started to spend so much time with Trudy. Anything not to be home and alone."

"Are you going to marry her?" I asked.

"Nope," said Dad. "Can't see that happening. Last thing in the world I want to do is take on another family."

"But I thought . . . you know."

"Forget it," Dad said. "No way I'm getting married again, and certainly not to Trudy. We don't get along all that well."

We turned a corner and Dad's apartment building was ahead. He turned into the parking lot and we went upstairs.

"Now, then," Dad said when we sat down in the living room, "how do we get to spend more time together? That's what we've got to figure out."

"Okay," I said. "I've been thinking, could you maybe come see me one night during the week?"

Dad thought about that, then said, "Maybe. We can try it and see how it works out. How's Wednesday night for you?"

"Wednesday night's good."

"Let's see, now," he said. "That means I'll have to drive straight over from whatever job I'm on. And we'll catch a bite somewhere close by. I can't keep you out late on a school night."

"I'm so happy," I said.

Dad laughed. "I guess I am too. Okay, so we'll have Wednesday nights together from now on."

"What about weekends?" I asked. "Could I maybe work with you on Saturdays? You know, be your helper and sleep over here?"

"I don't know," Dad said. "I move awfully fast when I'm working, and I don't know if you'll get in the way, Mark."

"I'll be very good," I said.

"You're already very good," Dad said. "What about Christmas week? Maybe you can try being my helper then, when I'm not so busy. We'll try and spend Christmas week together, just us two guys. Does that sound right to you?"

I didn't answer with words. I just jumped into Dad's arms and held on for dear life.

"Easy now," Dad said, breaking my embrace. He held me away from him. "Mark," he said, "if we're going to spend more time together, you've got to learn to see me as I really am, okay?"

"Sure."

"I try to do my best, but sometimes I'll forget. Or a job I'm doing turns out harder than I thought and I concentrate so hard on finishing it, I don't do two other things I'm supposed to do. Your dad is a forgetful kind of guy, okay? Sometimes he's unreliable, too, and I know I put my work ahead of other things a lot of the time. If you don't believe me, ask your mom and she'll tell you the same."

"I believe you," I said.

"So, babe, if I don't show up exactly on time or I forget to call you back it doesn't mean that I hate you or don't love you. It just means that Bill Baker is disorganized, as usual. But from here on I'm gonna try to remember everything that concerns you. And remember, I'm always thinking about you. Is that a deal?"

Dad put his big hand out and we shook. "Deal," I said.

29

COW-HAIR SOUP

After all those worst days of my life I think that Sunday might have been one of the best days. But only the second part of it, not the first.

It was like I'd had a big rock on my chest all along and suddenly someone lifted it off. I was sure of Dad now, that was the main thing. And I had something to look forward to, Christmas week when we'd be together. That seesaw I was on still kept going up and down, but now it spent a little more time in the middle.

Dad came over and took me out to dinner two Wednesday nights in a row. The first time we went to the Jade Garden and I introduced him to Joe and Mrs. Chang. Then the third week came along and Dad called me at the last minute and said he couldn't make it. He was hung up on a job, he said.

I put the phone down, very disappointed. But at least I knew Dad had a real reason for not coming. and it wasn't me.

"That father of yours," Mom said, shaking her head.

"Is great," I said. "And he works very hard." Mom didn't say anything more about Dad after that.

Joyce, Joe, and I finished our report on the children of Egypt. It turned out terrific and Mr. Pangalos gave us an A on it.

The week before Thanksgiving I was home after school. The doorbell rang and it was Minnie Olson. She had a tall plant in her hands. "Here I am going off to California and I almost forgot about my dracaena," she said. "Can I come in?"

"Sure."

Minnie followed me into the kitchen and put the plant on the sink. "I'm wondering if you could take care of my plant for me, Mark. I'm going to be away visiting my grandchildren for a couple of weeks."

"Okay," I said, "if you tell me what to do."

Minnie found a place for her plant near the window in my room and she said it had to be kept moist. "That doesn't mean soaking it, you know. Just a little water every few days. You got a watering can?"

"No."

"Then just give it a paper cup of water every few days. You got paper cups?"

"Yes."

"Good," said Minnie. "And, Mark, talk to my plant every once in a while so it doesn't get lonely, okay?"

I wasn't sure I'd heard Minnie right. "Talk to it?"

"Yes. I don't mean you to have long conversations. Just say hello and how are you doing, good morning and good night. Plants like that."

"I'll try to remember," I said. "When are you going to California?"

"Tomorrow morning. And I'm so nervous. I hate flying. How about you?"

"I don't mind it."

"Then you're braver than me," she said. "Did you hear about Phil Steinkraus? The juvenile court put him on a year's probation and he has to go for counseling twice a week."

"I haven't seen him in school," I said.

"Because he's been transferred to a middle school," Minnie said. "And they put him in a special class. Which is good, I think. Finally they're going to pay attention to him and maybe —God willing—they can straighten him out." Minnie looked down at her wristwatch. "Gotta go," she said, and headed for the door.

"Have a good trip," I said, "and a nice Thanksgiving. Don't worry, I'll take good care of your plant."

"That I know, you sweet thing," she said, and kissed my cheek. "And you have a good Thanksgiving too. Are you doing anything special?"

"Nope," I said. "It'll just be Mom and me."

On the way to school that Thursday Joe asked me what I was going to be doing for Thanksgiving. I told him the same thing I'd told Minnie.

Just after dinner that night the telephone rang. When I picked it up it was Mrs. Chang. She wanted to speak to Mom.

Mom and Mrs. Chang spoke for a long time. I heard Mom say "Thank you" a few times and "Are you sure?" And Mom said that she would make a pumpkin pie. So when Mom finally said good-bye to Mrs. Chang I knew what was coming. "We just got invited for Thanksgiving dinner by Helen Chang. How about that?"

"Great," I said.

"You told Joe we'd be alone, right?" she said. "And Joe asked his mom to invite us. He's really a very sweet boy, isn't he?"

"Joe?" I said. "Joe is the best."

I thanked Joe for the invitation the next morning. "But I thought the restaurant was going to be open," I said.

"Nope," said Joe. "It's one of the few days we're closed."

"Does your family have the regular things on Thanksgiving?" I asked. "You know, turkey and all that?"

"Of course not," said Joe.

"You eat Chinese food?"

"Not your everyday Chinese food," said Joe. "We'll have things you wouldn't believe."

"Like what?"

"It's a holiday," said Joe. "so we'll probably have snails' eggs . . . frog bottoms with pine cones . . . eye-of-newt pancakes . . ."

I stopped walking. "You're joking," I said.

"Absolutely not," Joe said. "I just told you what the appetizers will be. After that we'll have eel gizzard pie, roast pig tails, and the famous cow-hair soup."

I didn't want to hurt Joe's feelings, but it all sounded pretty awful to me. And I guess my face showed it.

All of a sudden Joe burst out laughing and I knew it was a joke. I chased him all the way to school.

30
TURKEY DAY

Mom spent the morning baking a pumpkin pie. I helped a little by breaking the eggs for her and reading out the recipe from the big cookbook. The pie looked fabulous when it was done and the whole apartment smelled wonderful.

Just after that Dad called to talk to me. He said he didn't have a job this coming Saturday and maybe the two of us could go fishing. I got all excited and told him I couldn't wait. Then I asked him what he was doing this afternoon, for Thanksgiving dinner.

"Oh, I have big plans," he said, laughing a little. "I'll probably have a ham sandwich and a bottle of beer and I'll watch two football games."

"You're not going to Trudy's house?"

"Nope," said Dad. He was quiet for a moment. "Looks like it's over between Trudy and me," he said. "I knew sooner or later that would happen . . . and it happened sooner."

"Then you'll be alone."

"Just me and my shadow," said Dad. "Don't worry about it, Mark. I'll be fine."

When we hung up, I couldn't help feeling sad. Thanksgiving always used to be such a happy holiday at our house. Now Dad was spending it alone.

I walked into Mom's bedroom. She was standing in front of her closet and looking into it, thinking about what clothes to wear. "Mom," I said, "I want to ask you a favor."

"Ask away," she said, moving a few skirt hangers around.

"I just got off the phone with Dad," I said. "He's going to be spending Thanksgiving all alone."

Mom turned to look at me and she seemed to know what I was about to ask. "Absolutely not," she said. "Your father can't come to the Jade Garden with us."

"But why not?" I asked. "It's not like it will only be the three of us."

"No," said Mom.

"I'm sure there'll be plenty of food. And Mrs. Chang probably wouldn't mind."

"Mark," Mom said, "I don't want to talk about it."

"But I do," I said, a little louder than I wanted to. "This is supposed to be a holiday, Mom. Families are supposed to be together on Thanksgiving. Don't you think I'd like to see both my parents sitting at the same table not yelling or screaming at each other? You could do that if you really wanted to. Will you please just think about it for five minutes before you say no?"

Mom folded her arms across her chest and walked over to the window. I followed a moment later and stood beside her. We could look out into the side street. It was very quiet, with no cars going by. On the porch of a small house across the street were two small kids dressed up in snowsuits. They were batting a Nerf ball back and forth to each other. Ears of Indian corn were hanging on the door of the house. As we looked on, the door opened and a woman in an apron stuck her head out and called something to the kids. They stopped what they were doing and ran inside.

I felt Mom's hand reach over and take mine. She sighed a couple of times.

"Let's see," she said in a husky voice. "I'll call Helen and ask if it's all right."

She sat down on her bed and called Mrs. Chang. When the phone call was finished, Mom nodded at me. "It's fine with Helen," she said. "But *you'll* have to call Dad and invite him."

"Right."

"And, Mark," she added, "I want you to know I'm doing this only for you."

"I know it," I said. "And thanks."

I ran off to the kitchen to call Dad. I thought he'd be so pleased, but in the end I had to talk him into it.

"This isn't your mom's idea," he said.

"What difference does that make?"

"Well . . . I don't know."

"Come on, Dad."

"If we end up fighting, it'll ruin everyone's day, Mark."

"Dad . . . please. It means a lot to me."

I heard Dad clear his throat. Then he finally said he'd come. "And, Mark, please tell your mom thanks for me."

Mom made her usual fuss about how clean I was and how my hair was combed. She recombed it herself, then put on some hairspray before I could stop her. She also tried on three different dresses from her closet before she found one she liked.

When Dad rang the downstairs doorbell I started getting nervous again. Could Mom and Dad actually spend a whole afternoon together without fighting? If they started screaming at each other in front of Joe and the Changs, I'd die.

I opened the apartment door for Dad. He stood there in the doorway, looking so different. His hair was combed down flat and neat for once, and he was wearing a dark suit with a white shirt and a tie. He looked as nervous as I felt.

"Hi, Joan," he said to Mom.

"Bill," said Mom. They looked each other over for a moment.

"You look very nice," Dad said to her.

"Why, thank you," Mom said.

"Is that a new dress?"

"It's an old dress," Mom said. "I haven't worn it in a long while, though."

"Well," said Dad, "you look really pretty in it."

"I'm glad you noticed," Mom said in an edgy voice.

I clenched my hands, expecting an argument to start. But Dad just smiled and shifted the paper bag he was carrying from one hand to the other.

"I . . . uh . . . brought a bottle of wine," Dad said.

"How nice," Mom said in a totally false way. "Shall we go?"

I slipped into my jacket and Mom put on her coat. She took the pumpkin pie and we went downstairs. It was very cold outside and the sky was a dirty gray color. Mom and Dad left

179

a space between them as we walked, and I filled it. Neither one said a word—they didn't even look at each other—and it got me scared. *Please behave,* I kept thinking, as if they were the children and I was the grown-up.

The restaurant had a CLOSED sign on the door, but Joe was there to open it for us. We got a big greeting from the Changs. Joe's dad wasn't wearing his apron for once, but was dressed in slacks and a white shirt. He shook hands with my dad and told him what a nice boy I was. Then Mishi came running up with a big yellow bow in her hair and Mr. Chang picked her up in his arms and introduced her to my dad.

Han was wearing slacks and a sport shirt, not his waiter's jacket and bow tie. "Turkey day," he said to me, smiling.

Dad gave Mrs. Chang the bottle of wine he'd brought and Mr. Chang took charge of Mom's pie. Then we all began to sit down at the big round family table, which had a pretty orange tablecloth on it. Dad held Mom's chair for her as she sat down. Then he motioned to me and I sat down next to her, with Dad on the other side of me.

Mrs. Chang brought out a big tureen of soup to begin the meal. Joe gave me a wink from across the table. "Ah, yes," he said, "the famous cow-hair soup," and we both started laughing.

Han came around the table and poured glasses of wine for everyone, including a few drops for Mishi. I was surprised when Mr. Chang tinged his knife against a water glass for attention, then stood up. "Thanksgiving is best holiday," he said, "family holiday. Thankful for my family, and thankful for good health." He took a sip of wine and sat down.

That's when Han stood up and made a toast. "Thankful

180

brother brings me here," he said, raising his wineglass. "Thankful for best country, America. Very thankful next year wife comes from Hong Kong."

Mr. Chang said something in Chinese to his brother and they both laughed. Then Mrs. Chang began to portion the soup into bowls to pass them around the table. When I got mine I inspected it just to make sure there wasn't a cow hair anywhere near it. It looked and smelled like vegetable soup.

Just then Mishi popped up. "I can do it too," she said, raising her glass. "I'm thankful for this very nice party," she began. "Parties are fun, especially birthday parties. I'm only sorry we had to kill the poor turkey."

Everyone laughed, and Mishi giggled and sat down.

We started eating our soup, which was delicious and had some strange vegetables in it. I began to think about what I could possibly say for a Thanksgiving toast of my own. *My family,* I'd say as I raised my glass, *I'm thankful that we're together, even for one afternoon. And I'm thankful that they're not being awful to each other in front of me.*

There was more I could say.

I'm thankful that I got my dad back . . . that he's not running away from me . . . that I'm sure of him again. And I'm thankful I found Joe and now he's my best friend. And I'm thankful for the other friends I'm starting to make in school . . . and to Minnie and the Changs for being so nice to me. And even though it sounds silly, I'm very thankful I got my bike back.

That would be my Thanksgiving toast, I guess. And maybe, for this year in my life, it was enough.

The next morning I got my bike out of the storage room and

went over to pick up Joe. We were going to Joyce's house to shoot some hoops. Joe unchained the delivery vehicle and we walked our bikes across Beverly Road. Then I hopped on my blue beauty and we both started pedaling off. The morning was cold, but very clear and sunny.

I shifted gears and pushed hard against the pedals, beginning to go faster and faster, the wind sharp across my face. At the next corner I looked back to see Joe far behind me. I stopped and waited for him to catch up.

Joe rolled up even with me and stopped his bike. "No way I can keep up with you on this old clunker," he said.

"Sorry about that," I said. "I'll slow down."

Joe nodded, staring at me. "You've got a big smile on your face," he said. "What's the joke?"

"No joke," I said with a shrug. "Just happy, I guess. Is there anything wrong with that?"

"Nope," said Joe, "not a thing. Happy is the way to be."

Then we started pedaling down the next street.

ROBERT KIMMEL SMITH is the award-winning author of many popular novels for children, including *Bobby Baseball, Mostly Michael, The War with Grandpa, Jelly Belly,* and *Chocolate Fever.*

He lives in Brooklyn, New York, with his wife, Claire. They have two grown children, Roger and Heidi.